Billy Craft

BY JAMES HUGHES

RoseDog Books
585 Alpha Drive, Suite 103
Pittsburgh, PA 15238
Visit our website at *www.rosedogbookstore.com*

ISBN: 979-8-89127-539-3
eISBN: 979-8-89127-037-4

BILLY CRAFT

Chapter One

The Craft farm located three miles south of town resided in in the southwestern part of the state. On the east face of the Appalachians it was a country of small rolling hills supporting small to medium farms. The southeastern sun light and the cool air flowing down the Appalachians invited the land to produce. The farm had been in the family for three generations. The barn had been constructed by the first-generation Craft in the early 1900s. Subsequent Craft men had cleared more timber to increase the usable acreage. As a working farm it produced oat grain for sale and vegetables and meat for the family and excess milk to sell to a wholesaler. The hay harvest also produced ample hay for their two cows and the excess was sold locally. George Craft the present owner with his wife Jenny and son Billy were the present occupants. George was a daylight to dark farmer; each day began with plan he had in his head resolute on what had to be done depending on the season. Jenny, his wife, was the family record keeper and Billy, his son, had his daily list of chores.

"Where's Billy" growled George Craft as he walked through the side door of the house into the kitchen.

"He probably had something left to do at school", answered Jenny.

"He knew I was going to cut the lower hay field tomorrow and I need his help to sharpen the cutter blade."

"Simmer down George, he will be along." Jenny promised.

George was not a man with a temper. Sometimes it just came out when he was disappointed. He had a schedule to do things and wanted them done on his schedule.

George and Jenny Craft worked the small farm that had been in the Craft family for three generations. George's father had died last year, and he was having a difficult time keeping the farm viable. He needed Billy's help now more than ever. George used to say about his father, when he dies it will take three men to replace him. But they did not have three men, it was just George and his son Billy doing the farm work. Jenny did her share taking care of the small vegetable garden and the chickens in addition to taking care of the house, the cooking and cleaning. She was also the family barber, cutting George's hair whenever she could corral him long enough for a 15-minute sit down; she also used to cut Mr. Craft's hair before he passed. She had cut Billy's hair too until he started high school. He wanted to look city instead of country as he said, and wanted to go to the barber in town. She and George enjoyed a small laugh about that.

The farm was originally built and developed by George's grandfather and then George senior increased the acreage to the present sixty-two acres. Two hay fields, an oat grain field, a barn and two milk cows, a chicken house plus the family house constituted the farm at present. There was also a shed where George kept most of his tools. George had recently bought five beef cattle with the hope of increasing the herd over time and making some money from new calves each spring.

A half mile away the principal prompting their brief exchange was pedaling furiously with his baseball glove dangling from the handlebars. Billy Craft was moving fast. His mop of brown hair flowing in the breeze except for a patch of hair flopped on his forehead darkened by the perspiration. Billy had always had his mother cut his hair short but the summer before he started to high school he had let it grow out. He remembered asking his mother before he started his freshman year if he could get a store-bought haircut before attending. His mother said smiling. "I think we can afford a quarter every month or so."

He had just turned on to the dirt and gravel road leading to the farm. It was beginning to turn dark, a part of the road he had pedaled before in complete darkness. At night his beacon was the large sycamore tree located about a quarter mile from home. That old sycamore with its white trunk glowing in the moonlight had been his beacon, like a vertical lighthouse when he traveled the road on a dark night. He knew his father would be angry at first because he was late. Sometimes he wished his father would give him ten licks with a willow branch rather than administering his scolding in short burst for 40 minutes.

He had stopped after school to play a few innings of pickup baseball with some friends. Having become involved in the play he had stayed longer than intended. As he pedaled along he thought about his ability to play sports like baseball and basketball. He was an average player, not the best, not the worst, just an average player. He did not like being average but his ability to shoot the ball or hit the ball rendered him average. "That's me average Billy Craft, ABC" he thought. He was not good enough to make the high school teams, he realized, so he did not even try out. One day he hoped to find something he was good at, not average but good. Perhaps he would be a good farmer like his father though that was not a life he aspired to.

He left the dirt and gravel road and headed up the dirt drive that led to the house and barn below. He hoped there would be time to help his father so they could finish with the cutter bar before dinner. He knew his mother had dinner prepared at a regular time each day and his father expected that.

Leaning his bike against the fence he hurried to the barn to find his father. His father ran the small 62-acre farm and did most of the real work. He did own a tractor to help with the hay cutting. Jenny worked managing the house and oversaw their finances. Billy too had chores that he faithfully performed, but he felt he was also entitled to do things other 16-year-old boys did.

"It's about time." George said as Billy came running into the barn

"Sorry Dad but we still have time to sharpen the cutter blade before dinner."

"Well then, start turning the crank on that stone wheel and let's get on with it."

The round stone's bottom third sat in a trough of water that as it turned kept the wheel wet and cool during the sharpening process. George told Billy the stone had been on the homesite before he was born. As Billy turned the crank on the stone wheel assembly his father held the blade points against the wheel to sharpen each tip. Turning the crank on the stone for 10 minutes and listening to his father's admonitions for being late he felt his arm would fall off, and possibly his ears too. At times he would switch to his left arm and turn for 10 minutes all the while receiving his father's scolding. As always, his father's anger subsided as the work progressed. It seemed the work took away the anger which was never loud or threatening just firm and just.

"So, what position did you play in the game today?"

"Third base Dad and I got two hits."

"How many errors in the field?"

"I guess about two got by me."

"You have to keep your head down and your eye on the ball you know." The anger was now completely gone, and the father emerged.

At times if George's agitation became too strident Jenny often stepped in to cool the waters. She had a way of tempering George and at the same time reminding Billy of his role on the farm. She could steer the conversation away from an unpleasant issue by bringing up an event or piece of good news that would cause George and Billy to pause, reflecting on her news. Jenny did not have a degree in psychology, but she knew the right buttons to push when necessary. It also did not hurt that she was terrific cook and sitting down at her table seemed the wrong place to have any thoughts except those associated with the present fare.

Jenny, full name Jennifer Evans Craft, first met George in late summer of 1942. He was in his army uniform, home on furlough, having been brought to the church social by his mother to show off her patriot son. Of course, everyone there had someone in, or knew someone who was in the military service at that time. George's mother walked him around introducing him to everyone she knew always patting him the back with each introduction. He awkwardly followed his mother enduring the process made more acceptable by the good things to eat offered him. Several young ladies were present increasing his interest, but he was too shy to make any connection until a young girl named Jenny introduced herself. Jenny had come down to the small southwestern Virginia hamlet from Charlottesville to spend the summer with her aunt preparing packages for service men overseas. These packages included razors, books, wool socks and sundry items not available to many overseas. It was being done all over America as acts of patriotism during the war. The church social was a reward for their efforts.

George was stationed stateside as a mechanic for all the army rolling stock, jeeps, trucks, halftracks, etc. He worked on them all. George was a little embarrassed that his mother paraded him around like he was General Patton, but he endured because of the several young ladies present. Jenny was the one that caught his eye and when she had introduced herself, he was suddenly glad his mother had brought him. He was not sure how to advance their conversation but Lucky for him Jenny was less inhibited and asked about how he liked the Army. That a least gave him something to talk about. Jenny had recently completed high school and was not yet sure what she wanted to do next. They got along very well, and George was surprised that a city girl would be friendly to him. After some more talking and some flirting they exchanged addresses. When George returned to base the regular correspondence became more than friendship. George started to be more conscious of how he dressed, and he knew his speech needed work. He planned to improve it now that he had met Jenny. Finally, when he received a 10-day furlough in February 1943 they married.

* * * * *

Summer would be here soon, and Billy's junior year would be behind him. His primary thoughts were to get a job for the summer and get a little cash in his pocket. He knew he could not ignore his work at the farm, and he planned to find a way to do both. He knew his mother and father loved the farm they had inherited from George's father and his grandfather before. He knew that someday the talk would include leaving the farm to Billy when they passed on. He dreaded that talk and hoped it was a few years off. It would be another example of average Billy Craft becoming average farmer Billy Craft.

Billy had lined up a summer job as stock boy at the local A&P Supermarket in town. As soon as school was out he would sit down with his father and mother and work out his schedule for farm work and his supermarket job. In his mind he would also find time to play some baseball with his friends on Sundays or after work ,or after farm chores by taking advantage of the added summer daylight. Billy always had good organizational skills which were reflected in his schoolwork. He was consistently on the honor roll, and was a regular B student with an A thrown in from time to time. He prided himself on being able to read his teachers. Noticing when a point or subject was emphasized, then knowing to look for a question or problem related to the teacher's emphasizes.

Sometimes when conversation at the dinner table became somber he would take the opportunity to tell of a good test score or recent good paper grade to improve the mood. He was not one to brag about his accomplishments, but it was important for his parents to know he was doing well in school.

Billy knew his father worried about the farm and how to keep it viable financially. He also wanted a good life for his family. The two milk cows produced more milk than the three of them needed and they had begun selling the extra to a wholesaler. They would put the extra milk in 5-gallon aluminum cans and Billy would haul them down by the mailbox at the foot of their driveway every other day for pickup. That was a consistent source of income, though small it contributed, and the milk would not be wasted. The two hay meadows they cut twice each summer was also in excess of the needs of their livestock and the extra was sold to local farmers. The oat grain from their small field was also sold as a favorite to those who had horses. Local farmers often called George about problems with their vehicles or farm equipment. All knew he could fix anything mechanical. For his help they worked out the cost or the barter for his service.

George, with Billy's help, kept up the daily farm routine until the hay was to be mowed. Then George hired a local man for two weeks during each cutting to pick up the hay and load it to the barn for winter storage or for sale. The hired man used an old flatbed pickup to carry the hay bales to the barn. George's 46 Ford pickup was also used and driven by Billy.

* * * * *

When he received the first paycheck Billy decided to take in a movie. But first after cashing the check he deposited most of the money in his savings account, keeping out enough for a movie or occasional bottle of pop. His friend Wayne Post also worked at the supermarket and decided to join him for a movie Saturday evening. That Saturday Billy pedaled his bike toward town excited to be seeing a movie and spending twenty-five cents for the movie and a box of popcorn. Wayne was waiting for him in front of the theatre. Billy leaned his bike against a lamp post next to Wayne's confident it would be there when they came out, no one would steal their bikes.

The movie was preceded by a short film showing college athletes running in track meets in California. They showed clips of various races at various distances, but the longer distance races caught Billy's attention. The announcer talked about the mile which was the premier event of the meet and went on to talk about Roger Bannister who had broken the 4-minute mile in 1954. These athletes were nowhere near Roger Bannister's mile record; the announcer was just making a historical reference. Billy did not even remember the movie or what it was about, but he had a glimmer of what he wanted to do. After the movie he told Wayne about his fascination with the track meet in the short subject movie. He was particularly interested in the mile event.

"Man, I could run the mile in times near what those guys did." he exclaimed

"Ha-ha you could not come within 3 or 4 minutes of their times. Those guys train for months every day to compete in those races. They are in prime condition." Wayne laughed

"I am in good condition. I have been pedaling my bike almost two miles twice a day for 3 years."

"You are not even close to the shape they are in." Wayne responded. Wayne was on the high school track team and though he did not run in the mile events he was familiar with those that did and how hard they worked.

"How fast did the winner run the mile in that event? Do you remember what the announcer said" Billy asked?

"I think it was 4 minutes and 35 seconds or something like that." Wayne recollected.

"I bet I could run the mile in 5 minutes right now." was Billy's response.

"Not even close, maybe 6 minutes, just maybe."

"Let's go over to the school track right now and you can time me."

"I don't have a stopwatch."

"Just use the second hand on your watch and time me."

They biked to the track. There was enough moonlight that they could see the track. Billy was a slender boy about five foot 7 and 135 pounds and with his bike riding and the work he did on the farm he felt he could run forever. Billy took off his shirt and did some stretches and some short warm up runs. When he was ready, he told Wayne to start him.

Wayne looked at this watch, gave the go signal, and Billy was off. He ran the first lap (four hundred meters) and looked strong. By the middle of the second lap he had started to slow. The slow down continued into the third lap. By the start of the fourth lap he was barely running and halfway through that last lap he was just walking.

"If you finish in the next 20 seconds you will have done 6 minutes and 30 seconds" Wayne yelled laughing.

"Kiss my ass. You were right it does take a different type of conditioning." Billy responded while gasping for air and sweating, even in the night air.

"But 6 minutes and 30 seconds for the mile is a starting point for me I guess."

"Guess again my track star friend. Four times around this track is only 1600 meters you need to add another nine meters to make a mile. There are 1609 meters in a mile."

"How do you know that?"

"I learned it in physics class when we were studying the metric system. There is also a metric mile which is 1500 meters"

"Oh shit, so the track team milers run 1600 meters in their meets. I have much to learn and a long way to go."

"Well, you seem to have motivation and that is always the first step in achieving a goal."

Chapter Two

Trying to get to sleep that Saturday night after the movie and his pathetic run he was conflicted. He was excited thinking about what he wanted to do and scared that it would be much more difficult than he had imagined. Before going to sleep he mapped out in his mind what he was going to do and how to proceed.

Two days later when he had some time he asked his mother if he could borrow the pickup for a little while. His father was off somewhere on the farm, so he had asked his mother. Billy had his driver's license and used the truck occasionally, mostly associated with farm related work.

"First let Wolley out and take these chicken scraps to Lilly and Liza." His mother responded.

Wolley was part Shepard, part who knows. Lilly and Liza were the two cats that lived in the barn. Wolley was Billy's dog they got for him when he was three. He came to them with the name Rolley but Billy at 3 had trouble with his "Rs" and the dog became known forever after as Wolley. Lilly and Liza were the offspring of George's mothers cat Amber. George always laughingly referred to Amber as the family tramp. Even though there were no male cats nearby Amber found herself pregnant and Lilly and Liza were the result. Wolley slept in the house at the foot of Billy's bed while Lilly and Liza occupied the barn. Each time Wolley visited the barn the two cats stood stiff legged glaring at Wolley. He was in their domain and both parties knew the rules long ago established. The standoff was short lived with Lilly and Liza turning away indignant.

"Fed your 2 granddaughters' mom." He said laughing as he led Wolley back to the house and called to his mom. "All done, I am leaving." He knew his mother would pick up on the bit of humor. She was always ready to smile at a clever quip. His father was slower, seeming to analyze a remark before deciding its humor content.

"We need to work patching that chicken coop again soon. I lost two hens this week to weasels and a skunk is getting in eating the eggs." She answered.

"Ok Mom, Sunday after church. I am going now."

With his mother's ok he drove the truck a half mile down their dirt road to the paved highway. He pointed the truck toward home and got out and took a stake he had made and pounded it into the ground on the side of the road directly across from the middle of the front wheel. This would be the start of his one-mile course. Then with an eye on the odometer he drove slowly until the odometer recorded a quarter of a mile. He got out and drove another stake by the side of the road directly across from the middle of the front wheel. That would be his quarter mile mark. He repeated this process at the half mile, three quarters, and full mile mark. Since he could not be sure of the accuracy of the measurements, he drove another stake ten yards beyond his mile mark as hedge against error. This would be the end of his mile run when he began his practice. Next, he knew he needed to buy a stopwatch. Being methodical he made up a chart with dates and a place for times for the various mile marks. The second half of the mile went past the farm. He wanted the mile layout to be all be on their gravel road.

He ran the course twice in the next 2 days, without a stopwatch, using his wristwatch to record the mile time. He had to get a feel for pace to go the full mile. He told Wayne what he had done and asked him to go with him to buy a stopwatch.

"I will run with you when I have time. It will help with my conditioning also though I do not care about mile times." Wayne offered

"Thanks, it will be good to run with someone for company and to help me with my pace." Billy responded.

"Billy here is some advice. When you begin you will find there is little or no improvement in your times for a while. Then one day when you are feeling good you will run and see your time improve by 7 or 8 seconds. That becomes your new benchmark. I learned this during my first two years running track. Times improve slowly but with continued practice they do improve."

"Okay coach good to know, thanks." laughed Billy

"Then you are really determined to do this, practice regularly?" Wayne asked.

"Of course, I am determined. I am tired of being average Billy Craft. I will be on the track team with you next spring and I will run the mile, or 1600 meters."

"Well then I have a recommendation."

"Okay coach let's have it."

"You should go out for the cross country team this fall. It is much different than the mile run but it will strengthen your legs particularly the calf muscles because the cross-country runners run up hills that are long and steep. It will be good for conditioning, and it will involve competition."

"Sounds like a good idea but If I run, I will run to win."

" Whoa, hot shot some of these guys have been running cross country for four years and they know how to run the hills and pace themselves."

"Good advice, I will go out for cross country. The competition will be something I need."

* * * * *

"What are all those stakes you have placed along our road?" Billy's father asked one evening. He called it our road though it was a public road used by a few others.

"It is a course I have laid out to measure a mile. I plan to go out for track next spring and run the mile for our school."

"Really? That is something new", Billy was afraid he was now going to get a lecture on how he could run track and still do all his farm duties.

"How did you lay out the mile?"

"I used the odometer on the truck."

"That can't be very accurate."

"Yes, I know, but it was the only way I could think to do to it."

"Your uncle Roy is a surveyor. We could have him come and lay it out accurately someday."

Billy could not believe what he was hearing. He had expected a lecture and now he was hearing his father endorse his plan.

"That would be great Dad. Do you think he would?"

"Well, if I invited him and Peggy over for one of your mother's Sunday dinners I think we could persuade him to bring his surveying equipment." George laughed.

"Wow, it would be great to have an accurate layout."

"Now let's go break the news to your mother that we are having company for Sunday dinner." His dad laughed.

Billy did not think he had ever had such a welcome surprise. He would have an accurate mile, layout but the best surprise was the attitude of his father. To Billy Christmas had come early this year.

On Sunday before dinner his new course was laid out by his Uncle Roy and Billy repositioned his stakes. He had been surprisingly close to Uncle Roy's mark. His dad, with his uncle watching, said for him to run the mile and he would hold the stopwatch. Then his dad drove him down to the starting point, gave Billy the go, and started the stopwatch. His dad drove ahead to the finish line to record his time. He knew he had to pace himself to make sure he would finish. He did not want to be embarrassed in front of his dad and uncle. Looking up panting hard as he finished, he said. "How was it."

"I have recorded your time. In a month I will record you again and see if you have improved."

"You are not going to tell me time today?"

"If I keep it a secret you will assume you have not done well and will be motivated to work harder."

"I guess I hadn't heard about your receiving a psychology degree George." Roy laughed.

"I call it common sense. Now do we still want to argue over times and philosophy, or do we want to go eat some of Jenny's cooking?"

With his newly laid out mile Billy tried to run it 3 or 4 times each week and recorded his times. Some day he would ask to see the time his father had recorded. He also tried to record his times at the quarter mile marks by looking at his watch when he passed each and remembering the time. As he thought about each quarter's recordings he decided that was silly since he did not know what times were expected for the various quarters. He would have to wait to be in competition before that had any relevance.

Every week or two his father would take the time to record his time but would never tell him. The fact his father was there was all of the motivation he needed to try harder on those days. The times were not as important as his father's interest.

In the fall he did go out for the cross country team along with Wayne.

"Remember Billy in cross-country low score wins." Wayne offered, knowing that would throw Billy.

"Yea right, just like in baseball, basketball, football the one with the lowest score wins, last place." Billy responded smartly.

"No, low score is first not last. Think about it. As each runner finishes his position is recorded. The team with runners finishing soonest have the lowest numbers and when added up are the winners."

"Damdest think I ever heard. Only in cross-country."

"Well, there is also golf. You country boys should get out into the world more." Wayne was laughing.

"Since you will always be running behind me, kiss my ass," was Billy's response.

His friend was right when he said this cross country was much different than running on a flat track. Those runners knew how to pace themselves and how to run the ups and downs of a cross country course, but he did enjoy the competition. Regardless of where he was in the race it was always good to see if he could pass the runner in front of him. In the last 2 or 3 meets of the season he did run well enough to earn a few points for the team. Wayne was also right about the calf muscles. Running some of those hills his legs ached like he never imagined.

Chapter Three

"Good afternoon. Welcome to the first day of track practice. I am Mr. Barnes, your coach. We have much to discuss today but first everyone take two laps around the track for warm up. No sprinting, I do not want pulled muscles the first day; Just do a slow jog."

They were on the athletic field just below the school where football and other sports were played. A four-hundred-meter track circled the field. The building of Hilton High School was above the field and was a 2-story brick building in the shape of a U. The two legs of the U enclosed the gymnasium between. Like most high school gymnasiums, it served a multi-purpose function, as gym for athletics, as the basketball court, for school proms and other social events. Classes for juniors and seniors were on the top floor while the bottom level served the freshmen and sophomores. Two wide sets of cement steps led from the school front down to the athletic field where the track team had gathered for the start of spring training.

Everyone took off together, including non-runners like high jumpers, discus throwers, etc. Billy and Wayne jogged together. The day was one of those early spring warmups, one that delivers 80-degree weather for 2 or 3 days and then reverts to temperatures predicted in the almanac. All were thankful he emphasized jog not run. Because of recent inclement weather most athletes had not been running and so conditioning was an issue. That coach's admonition against running would only have been better if he had said walk, or better yet no laps today. Billy was looking for Jack Wells and Ben Avery. Jack was tall and slender, 2 or 3 inches taller than Billy. It was obvious he was carrying no excess weight. Ben was about Billy's size and weight but more muscular. He knew they were milers from the previous year and was acquainted with them since he had classes with both. He would pick their brain about Coach Barnes and what to expect. Billy spotted Jack and Ben running together and moved up close to them.

"Hey guys, how is it going? I decided to try to run the mile this year with you two," was Billy's way of introducing his intent.

"Hi Billy, nice to see you here. Why did you wait for your senior year to try out?" Jack responded

"Well to be honest I saw a movie short subject of Roger Bannister breaking the 4-minute mile, and got interested by that I guess."

"So, you are out to break the four-minute mile in high school?" Jack laughed.

"Well, it might take a week or two to do that. What do you think?" Billy said while laughing. All four boys could not stop laughing.

"Bad news Bill we don't run the mile, we run the 1600 meters." Ben advised still laughing.

"Even if you run the 1600 meters in 4 minutes you will not break the 4-minute mile since the mile is about 9 yards longer than the 1600 meters." Ben reminded him.

"Good to know, yes Wayne told me. I am not worried about breaking records I just want to know what it will take to make the team?" Billy asked

"Well, if you beat me and Ben you will make it." Jack responded

"You guys will have to teach me how to race. I know how to run but I do not know the first thing about racing, the tactics you know."

"You will learn. Coach Barnes is good about teaching tactics for a race."

"By the way what is the school record here for the 1600 meters?" Billy asked

"I think it is about 4 minutes 28 seconds and neither of us have done that." Ben added

"But Ben, now we have Roger." Jack laughed again.

They continued the jog, trading banter and talking about the upcoming season, coasting to a stop where Coach Barnes was standing with his clipboard.

"Okay everyone, take a knee. I want to go over some things. I have your names and the event you signed up for, but I reserve the right to put you in the event I think is best for the team. You will be given the opportunity to try for your desired event, but the needs of the team come first. Today I will be dividing you into three groups. Mrs. Holmes will work with the sprinters and hurdlers; Mr. Bennett will work with the field event members, and I will be with the distance runners. Now everyone get with your group."

Assembling with the milers Coach Barnes gave his instructions. He would address the other distance groups separately. "We have five milers signed up and I will only be entering 2 or 3 in each meet. All five are part of the team and each week will have the opportunity to be a starter for the upcoming meet. The same goes for the 800 and 800 relays, also the 400s; I will keep 2 or 3 for each event. Let us start with the milers first. I want you to run four laps when I say go. I will not be timing you today but every run starting tomorrow will be timed. I just want to see if you can run the distance today, see who has been working out and getting ready for the season.."

The five boys who had signed up for the mile took off at the coach's signal. Billy was not sure how to pace himself when running with the others, so he just decided to shadow Jack and Ben. He would attempt to stay close but would not try to pass them even if he felt he could. The first three laps were run at an even pace but starting with the final lap both Jack and Ben increased their speed. Billy stayed just behind them and felt good that he was able to stay close. The two underclassmen had fallen several yards behind. They finished with Jack in first, Ben second, and Billy just a yard behind Ben.

"Billy, or should I call you Roger, you did well, how do you feel? Jack said while panting when they finished and walked the cool down lap together.

"I feel okay. I was just trying to watch you and Ben and keep pace." Billy responded out of breath.

"Billy Craft you need to work on your arms and arm action." Coach Barnes called out

"My arms, what's wrong with my arms?"

"The arms are especially important when running. When the arm action gets lazy you can tell a runner is tiring. You will need to do some weight training and arm exercises." Coach answered.

That was a first for Billy. He had never even thought about his arms when running, but if his coach said to work on his arms that is what he would do. Billy had a growth spurt this past year and was about 5 ft. 9 in. and a hundred fifty pounds. He felt stronger after last fall's cross-country season.

Coach Barnes had built a reputation in developing winners at Hilton high school. He had taken over the track team coaching 8 years ago. He also taught geometry at the school. The last 4 years his runners had done very well at the regional and state meets. They had won several events where they were considered the underdogs, particularly in the distance races. He was able to get his runners up at the right time for the big meets. Some coaches from other teams were skeptical about his methods.

Coach Barnes and his wife who also taught at Hilton high school had done very well for themselves financially. He bought a new car every two years and just this year they had moved into a bigger and finer house. They had two incomes, and he received an additional stipend for coaching the track team. So, their investments appeared to have gone very well. His reputation as a successful track coach was also spreading.

Chapter Four

The next two weeks the milers were timed every day. Their times were unchanged for a few days. Then one day they would post a time 4 or 5 seconds better than their best. Maintaining that improvement was the goal and more improvement was hoped for. The first meet with an opposing high school was 10 days away and coach Barnes was pushing them hard. Billy had been able to stay with Ben and some days beat him by a step or two, but Jack was always the leader, though Billy had shortened the time between them.

"You have to pump those arms Billy" Coach Barnes repeated it seemed every day.

Billy worked every day before practice with arm curls and the heavy rope making it dance like a sine wave. A full minute with that rope made both arms feel like they would drop off. Coach was also telling them to load up on carbohydrates in their diet. Billy was not about to suggest to his mother what to fix for their meals. What his mother put on the table was what the three of them ate. His father worked hard each day and her meals were geared to what he needed. He did start to pay attention to foods with high carbohydrates and took extras helpings.

Billy's decision to run track was approved by both his mother and father, but he often got home too late to be of the help his father needed. He still did his morning chores before leaving for school, including milking their two cows. His mother had taken a part time job as a bookkeeper for a hardware store in town. This extra income allowed them to hire a man part time to help with farm work. She only had to be away from the house one day a week when she went to the store and gathered up the receipts for the week and updated the books. His mother had been keeping the books for the farm for years and she knew how to fill out a ledger.

Ever since he had laid out his track last summer and then joined the cross-country team he knew he was stronger. There were times in practice when Billy felt if he really pushed it he could beat Jack to the line, but felt that might produce a rift in his relationship with Jack, and with the team. The team looked upon Jack as their star. One day maybe, not yet.

One day each week was planned for sprint training. They would pretend a lap was the last in a 4-lap race and that lap would be run with a designated plan. Coach wanted them to be begin this simulated last lap running at a pace faster than normal, then with about 150 yards to go he would yell to increase the pace and with fifty yards to go he would call for an outright sprint, as hard as they could run. Jack's long legs consistently produced the winner at the finish line. Billy had been thinking about a strategy in this practice event. When the next sprint-training day was planned, usually a Thursday, he would try his strategy. His plan was to begin at the 150-yard mark when the pace was increased and stay right on Jack's shoulder hoping to make him run harder than normal early, then during the all-out sprint he hoped Jack would have less kick left. The following Thursday he tried the maneuver and though Jack still won the sprint Billy was only about a half step behind.

"What the hell was that all about?" Jack asked after the run.

"Just trying to win; isn't that what I am supposed to do?"

"So, you are finally figuring out how to race, not just run. Good for you." Jack was not upset with him at all, and that was good.

The day of the first meet had arrived, a Friday. It was a tri-meet among Hilton, Fairland Consolidated, and Wellesley high schools. The meet would be at Fairland Consolidated so Billy and the team would travel there in a school bus. It was in the same county about twenty-two miles away. Fairland Consolidated had a miler named Art Wells who had come in second last year at the state meet, and he was the obvious competition to beat. Jack had raced against Wells last year and knew he was good, but Jack felt he had a flaw. Billy had grabbed two bananas at lunch time hoping that would be enough carbohydrates to help him run well. He ate one at lunch and saved the second to eat before the race.

"Jack, you raced against Wells and you know he always likes to be out front." Coach Barnes reminded him.

"Yes, I know. I do not know if it is an ego thing with him or whether that is where he is comfortable." Jack added.

"We might be able to take advantage of that and make him feel less comfortable. Ben has a hamstring pull and will not be running, so it is just you two in the mile," indicating Jack and Billy, Barnes went on.

"The two of you need to take runs at him during the race. Jack, run up to him acting like you intend to pass and get him to increase his pace, then back off after a few yards. Then Billy you make a run at him, get right on his outside shoulder forcing him to increase his pace. Do this a couple of times during the race and let us see if we cannot tire him out for his final kick." Coach Barnes exposed his strategy.

The race went as planned and there was some success in the tactic, but Art Wells won the race. Jack and Billy finished in almost a dead heat one yard behind, Jack getting second over Billy with his lean at the tape. Both Jack and Billy recorded their personal best at 4 minutes 31 seconds.

Billy's mom was waiting for him in the pickup when they arrived back. On the drive home he told her about the race and how close he had been to winning. He was excited and told his mother he could not wait until the next race.

"Were you nervous before the race?" She said driving home.

"I was. My underarms were pouring sweat The waiting around before they called us was pure torture. The milers are the last to run, so we just rooted for the others in their events."

The practice he had put in running the track he created, and the cross-country work was starting to pay off. It was after 9 when they got home and to his surprise his father was still up to greet him. He went to sleep that night thinking the best part of his day was having his father still up to greet him.

Billy knew he was improving each week. He was less tired after the timed event each day and his sprinting had improved. In the fourth meet, against Western High, he won the race and beat Jack by a full yard. Coach Barnes had been watching the improvement and now thought of Billy as his lead runner in the mile, but he still felt an obligation to Jack who had been in the program 4 years.

Chapter Five

To say that Harrell Forsythe was born on the other side of the tracks was an oversimplification of his upbringing. At almost six foot and 160 pounds with dark hair like his mother he was handsome and always full of life. His large home was a long way from the railroad tracks and the accompanying train whistles and roaring locomotive sounds. Hs grandfather had grown up close to the tracks and loved the sounds of the railroad. He had served 30 years as superintendent there, but his wife hated the noise, so he built them a house on fifty acres of land about five miles from the tracks.

Harrell's father, Martin, grew up working summers on the tracks, but opted for law school and an easier way of life. The old house had been enlarged to accommodate the grandfather and grandmother as well as Harrell's mother and father and their children. It was where Harrell and his sister, Amy, began life. The original fifty acres became in time a 150-acre working farm. Harrell's father Martin met Doris in college and when both graduated, they married. Martin began the practice of law with a local 3-man firm. Doris became a college professor in literature.

After the initial growing process with the firm Martin developed a proficiency in dealing with large firms. He became successful in attracting larger companies to choose their firm for legal representation. After a few years he became efficient in representing one company suing another. This increased the 3-man firm's prestige, and it became a very successful.

Martin was appointed managing partner and with the prestige came money and wealth for his family. The additional work required the hiring of more lawyers, and the firm grew. He invested in and increased the farm buying a herd of beef cattle. He became well known for his Angus herd and the breeding stock. That became his featured interest when not at work. He studied the care and breeding of beef cattle and became noted expert in that field. His interest in golf and tennis waned, though for the family's sake he still maintained his membership in the local country club.

Martin's father, William, grew up doing hard work around the rail hands. Hard work was all they knew. As a young boy he spent his summers working with the track hands, mostly bringing them water. As he got older and bigger he worked alongside the others listening to their tales and jokes. It was an education he could never get in school, learning when the right time to plant corn by the sign of the moon, when was the best time to pick apples for the best cider. These men never aspired to be bosses or supervisors; their motivation was not in personal advancement but in pursuing their life with their family and with each other, hunting, fishing, and playing cards on Saturday night. They ribbed each other unmercilessly about anything they thought dumb. Even when he became superintendent William still enjoyed the company of the rail workers. Grandfather Forsythe was the rebel of the family. He was the first to tell an off-color story or joke at the kitchen table, something he heard from the railroad workers. Martin would scowl at him which meant tone it down dad. William being a railroad man was a hand on the throttle and foot off the brake kind of man. Thus, Harrell and his siter Amy were initiated into Grandfather Forsythe's world and it was where Harrell got his love for humor. At times that penchant for humor got him in trouble. In elementary school he wrote a love letter to his teacher and signed another boy's name. The prank, soon discovered, bought him a trip to the principal's office and a letter home. After the proper apologizes he returned to class. He did become the most popular boy on the playground as a result. All flocked to him except Jason Adkins, the initially accused, whose idea of humor still lay dormant. Harrell's grandfather was the only family member who thought it funny. "Please Dad don't encourage him," was Martin's reply.

Martin was expected to work hard around the tracks growing up also and though his father was railroad superintendent he was shown no favoritism. It was a trait Martin passed on to Harrell. They had a working farm and Harrell was expected to contribute. He worked daily during the summers with the farm hands and was expected to get his hands just as dirty as the others. On weekends when he was not at his law office Martin was out on the farm working also. That was his release from the legal world. It was the Forsythe way, instilled by the grandfather. If something needs to be done, do it, do not wait for others.

Harrell's DNA was an amalgamation of all the family members, intelligence from his mother, hard work from his father, and a sense of humor from his grandfather. For years while still in elementary school Harrell worked alongside his grandfather on the farm, who by then had retired, and who constantly reminded Harrell he was no better than the farm hands. His grandfather's lessons he embraced as a way of life.

Harrell and his older sister Amy were also introduced to the finer things in life which included golf and tennis lessons at the country club, and education in private schools. As his high school age approached Harrell decided he wanted to go to a local public high school. He had grown up playing with boys in the area which included sons of people who worked at the railroad and on the farm. Harrell never thought of himself as better than those boys whose fathers worked for his family. He felt comfortable with them. His parents relented and enrolled him in the local high school.

He was a naturally gifted athlete and pursued all activities available to him. He had great self-confidence and wanted to excel at everything. He always wanted to win no matter the activity. Amy, two years older than Harrell, used to beat him regularly in tennis. To remedy that he took additional tennis lessons 3 or 4 days a week. Finally, he was able to beat her. Not every time, but enough to give him satisfaction.

Those that did not know him well thought of him as cocky and a smart ass, but those that knew him well knew it was just his self confidence that burst forth whenever there was something to overcome. The one sport he did not pursue was football, other than to play pickup ball in the farm field or the in yard. He felt the grind of 3 hours a day for 5 or 6 days in the hot sun for a chance to play maybe a few minutes on Friday night was a poor investment of his time.

Harrell could always run, and when he first started track practice in high school he applied to compete in the middle-distance races, like the four hundred meter and 800-meter races. His style was to run from behind other runners then make a fast kick and pass them to win. He did not do it to embarrass other runners it was just his style. Some who did not know him well thought it was just an ego thing, but at the end of the race he was always friendly and congratulatory to the other runners.

After his freshman year he decided he wanted to run in the longer distance races. The longer races would allow him to analyze those ahead of him, to judge their pace, and to plan when he could pass them. Starting his second year he became a miler (1600 meters). He loved the strategy of running and planning as he ran. The multi-lap races allowed him to plan his moves, when to make them, and who was his biggest competition. He relished the challenge and by his senior year he was almost unbeatable in the scheduled meets that year. The 1600 meters race suited his personality. One day he decided he would run the mile in the Olympic games. It was a goal he sat for himself.

His grades in school were always been excellent and college had always been the plan of his father and mother. His father wanted him to study medicine and had made plans for him to attend one of the best universities, but Harrell was not sure what he wanted to do as an adult. At present running in the Olympics was the goal he had set for himself. He was always telling that to his friends but not to his parents.

At times while sleeping he dreamed about being in the Olympics. Sometimes the dreams were disjointed like most people's dreams. All the elements were there, the people, the places, the excitement, but the dreams at times would go in directions unrelated to his Olympic running. He thought his dream brain contained all the colorization of the race but would then go to random and strange unrelated pictures. But he had one recurring dream that followed a very logical progression, just like a real race. He would be running hard with a competitor just a half step ahead of him and suddenly the dream ended. He invariably woke up and lay there breathing heavily out of breath. Did he lose that race? There was no ending and it bothered him from time to time. He seemed to have that dream after a particularly hard practice or a difficult track event. He needed to find out what was causing this dream.

During his senior season Harrell had won the 1600 meters in every event he had entered. Local papers and even some statewide had touted him as the odds-on favorite to win the state championship. Harrell with his usual confidence was not about to disavow that assumption. "I should be able to break the state high school record too if I don't have an injury," This was not said in a boastful way, it was just Harrell being confident. Thus was his frame of mind as the regional meet neared, only 10 days away. He had also changed his running tactics instead of running from behind and then kicking to pass everyone he decided he would lead the race the whole way. He would let runners get close then increase his pace to stay in front. It was not an ego thing it was just the challenge he enjoyed.

Chapter Six

There was only one more track meet before the regionals. Jack had been training hard with extra determination. He was running extra sprints each day and had a new mindset. Billy knew it was partly because he had beat Jack in the last race. Coach Barnes was viewing Billy or Jack as their best chance to do well in the regional meet and to qualify for the state event, 2 weeks after the regional.

"Man, your kick lately has been something. Have you been loading up on carbohydrates?" Billy laughed talking to Jack.

"No, it is just that this is my senior year and I want to qualify in the regional and finally go to the state meet." Jack responded.

"I would like to qualify also. Is it possible for both of us to do that?"

"They will take the 4 best regional times, so yes both of us could qualify."

In the final track meet before the regionals, against Jackson High, an unfortunate event occurred. In the final fifty meters of the 1600 Billy was leading Jack and another runner when out of the corner of his eye Billy saw Jack gaining on him and beginning to pass him. He could feel the heat from Jack's body as they were abreast. With a final push Jack lunged for the finish line, won by a half step, and fell forward on the track right on his face. Gasping for air Billy went to help Jack up. He could not stand without help and was grabbing his right hamstring. Billy helped him up and started rubbing his leg.

"Quit." Yelled Jack

"I am just trying to help with your cramp."

"It is not a cramp. I felt something pull in my right leg."

"Jack, they said you broke the school record for the 1600, actually we both did, but it is your record alone by .25 seconds."

The team doctor took over the examination of Jack and later that evening Billy learned he had pulled a ham string. There would be no more running for Jack. Billy would be the lone entry for Hilton High School in the upcoming regional meet.

Monday's practice getting ready for the regional saw Jack come to practice on crutches.

"Man, I am so sorry for what happened Jack. I wanted both of us to have a chance to qualify for the state event. You would have been our lead runner; you won more races this year than me."

"Well, I went out with a bang, right on my face." Jack answered with a wry smile.

"It's going to be up to you now my friend to represent Hilton the rest of the year."

"Without you there to help me with my pace it won't be the same."

"You are going to be running against a guy from down state who has won all his races this year and is favored to win the state championship. A guy named Harrell Forsythe who they say is a real "hotdog"."

"What do we know about him?"

"They say he likes to be out front, always with a smile as if tempting others to pass."

"I know coach Barnes will have some ideas of how I should run, but I want your advice on how to beat him. Help me plan a strategy."

"Okay, we will talk about it this week."

Billy worked extra hard all week. He especially wanted to improve the length of his final sprint, with a strong-arm action. He normally would start his sprint with about fifty meters to the finish line. That week he worked on increasing it to about 60 or 65 meters. He reasoned he would have to start the sprint earlier against this Forsythe guy. He conferred with the coach and Jack about strategies.

"Jack, coach Barnes has given me some ideas; what do you think I should do strategy wise?"

"Well from what I hear this guy Forsythe is exceptionally good. It will take your best to beat him."

"You say he likes to run up front. Should I stay close to him?"

"I have been thinking that you should stay middle of the pack for 1200 meters and then close on him a bit. Get close and cause him to increase his pace before he is ready to do so, then back off but stay close. Do that 2 or 3 times, maybe you can force him out of his rhythm. It is all of I can think of to try. Remember we used that strategy earlier in the year at a meet."

"At least it is a plan and sounds better than anything I can come up with. I am too nervous to think straight."

The rest of the practice week he continued to work extra hard and formulated in his mind Jack's strategy. He also loaded up on carbohydrates all week. As he lay in bed each night he went over the strategy Jack had proposed. He did not want his mind cluttered with strategy during the race. He just wanted it to be automatic and feel when the time was right to make his moves. The team travelled to the site of the regional meet which was to be held on a junior college track to negate any homefield advantage for any of the runners.

As always the 1600 meters was to be the last race of the day. Billy hung out with Jack, still on crutches. Harrell Forsythe was pointed out to him early on which only increased his nervousness. He was a good-looking boy with an athletic body who seemed at ease watching the other events. Billy and Jack talked over the strategy and hoped it was the right approach to beating the favorite. Finally, it was time.

There would be eight runners in the event all of whom had been the best at their schools. The four with best times would qualify for the state track event. At the state meet they would be running against other regional qualifiers. At the standing start all were ready and the gun sounded. All eight took off in a sprint trying to get a close inside position during the first 30 or 40 meters. Soon all settled into a position, Billy in the middle of the pack, with Harrell Forsythe racing to the front. Billy ran with ease and had no trouble staying with the middle group. He watched ahead at Forsythe to see if he could see any chink in his armor. Forsythe raced easily with confidence. After the third lap Billy started to move up. He came right up just a yard from Forsythe's right shoulder causing him to glance at him and increase his pace to stay in front, then Billy backed off about 3 or 4 meters. He applied his strategy two more times hoping he had caused the leader to worry about him. Finally, with about 50 or 60 meters to the finish Billy began his sprint as did Forsythe. They left the rest of the runners several meters back. It was a mad race to the finish line for the two of them. With about ten meters to go the two of them were side by side, both at maximum effort. They stayed that way until the finish with Forsythe winning by half meter. Billy laid down more exhausted than he had ever been. He was still seated gasping for air when Harrell Forsythe came over to him and sat down beside him.

"Hello, I am Harrell Forsythe. You are the best I have ever run against, great race man."

"Thanks." Was all Billy could get out, still gasping for air.

"You scared me man, I thought you were going to beat me until the last step. I was fortunate to win. What is your name?"

"Billy, Billy Craft is my name from Hilton High."

"I would like to know how you train. That was some last fifty meters; I never had to work that hard to finish a race. We should get to know each other."

"It looks like we will be seeing each other again in the State Meet in 2 weeks." Billy reminded him, finally breathing normally.

"Yea, you are right. Now I will not be able to sleep nights thinking about running against you." Harrell laughed.

"I too will have sleepless nights." Billy responded.

They got along so well that they spent the next hour or so talking about everything. Harrell, it turned out, was a very gracious winner. He continually complimented Billy on his race. He was not the hotdog Billy had heard. Billy liked him.

* * * * *

Two more weeks of training and the State Track Meet was here. Billy thought about Harrell often during the 2 weeks. He was looking forward to seeing him, at the same time nervous about racing him again. Billy could think of no strategy for this race. He would just try to stay close to the leaders and hope he could prevail at the end. In 4 minutes plus his high school career would be over he thought; it had seemed to go by so quickly and he had no idea what was next.

The final 1600 would include eight runners with best times from their regionals. Billy knew they would all be good, that is why they were here. Waiting through all the other events was agonizing for all the runners and it was no different for Billy and Harrel. Waiting during the other events they smiled and acknowledged each other with a wave but they did not talk. Billy felt his mouth was too dry to talk and wondered if Harrell felt the same. Finally, it was time. All gulped their final deep breath. The runners took their position and the gun sounded.

At the starting gun all 8 runners sprinted for position. There was just a single pack, all eight staying within 1 or 2 yards of the front runner. Harrell was in the front by about a meter and Billy and another runner was on his right shoulder. Slowly those three pulled away from the others at about the 1000-meter mark. Now it would be a fight to the finish among those three. There was some strategic jockeying back and forth for the lead and all three looked strong. The final fifty meters was a dead heat sprint, all three abreast. Harrell was to Billy's left, and they were dead even. The runner to Billy's right was a half-step behind and Billy could see only his left arm as he pumped to get closer. He could feel the heat from both their bodies. There was no thought of looking left or right as that would ruin his momentum; he just focused on the end line and ran. Billy reached down for all he had with his eyes darting left and right at his competition, no head movement. Straining with his last ounce of energy he leaned for the tape. At the finish he won with his lean over Harrell and the third runner, but he was not sure until they announced it.

Collapsing on the ground for air Billy was beyond exhaustion. The thought of his win had to take second place to breathing. He was hoping there was enough air in the stadium to fill his lungs. Harrel was three yards away prone, also breathing hard. He said later he felt like a goldfish that had been dumped out of his bowl gasping for oxygen.

With a big grin Harrell wrapped his arm around Billy's shoulder.

"Congratulations man you did it, great race."

"Thanks." Billy gasped. "You too."

"That's the most fun I ever had racing." Harrell laughed.

"Fun? What are you a masochist?"

"It's the competition, that's what I love, always have."

"In about a week when I catch my breath maybe I will enjoy it also crazy man." Billy laughed at him.

After congratulations from the other runners Billy was starting to think this was the greatest thing that ever happened to him, then he stood up and faced the stands to see his mother standing and clapping; sitting beside her was his father with a smile and a little wave. Now it was the best thing that ever happened to him. No longer just average Billy Craft.

Chapter Seven

Billy and Harrell had had an almost instantaneous relationship starting with the regional meet; it continued during their confrontation in the State Track Meet. After the battle they had shaken hands and began to talk. They were kindred spirits, and especially Harrell who acted like he had never had a close friend before and seemed to need one. They had exchanged phone numbers and promised to stay in touch during the summer.

Frequent phone calls during the summer never seemed to lack subjects to talk about. They talked about running of course and about college, with Billy not sure of his college plans and Harrell being groomed by his father to attend some prestigious university. They spoke of home and family life and marveled at their differences. When Billy initiated the call his mother would frequently have to remind him he had been talking for about an hour, time to wrap it up.

Harrell had been asking Billy to visit him for a few days, which sounded exciting to Billy but with the trepidation that he would feel out of place visiting a home that he knew would be grander than anything he was accustomed to experiencing. More important was the work he would be missing on the farm and how his father would react. Also, his fulltime job at the supermarket would require some juggling. Working overtime for several days could allow him a few days off. With Harrell's constant pleading for a visit Billy conferred with his mother about the trip. He was worried about his table manners and the clothes he would wear and whether he would come off as a country bumpkin to Harrell's family. Jenny told him to be polite, no elbows on the table, and thank the Forsythe's for their hospitality. He would be fine she said. She said he had some nice summer clothes that she would iron up and he would not be embarrassed. His mother was instrumental in convincing his father that Billy needed to go. "He needs to get out into the rest of the world" she said. Finally, the next time Harrell asked he agreed to come for a few days whenever it was convenient for them both. His mother helped him select and pack his best clothes. Billy was excited but also nervous.

Harrell met Billy's bus overjoyed to see him again. During the ride to the house, Harrell driving, they joked and teased each other as if they had only parted yesterday.

"So now you are a big boy and your mother let you ride the bus all by yourself? Laughed Harrell. Humor was Harrell's second language. Billy enjoyed a good joke or a story but was a little more circumspect in his approach.

"Yes, she advised me not to talk to strangers and to put my wallet in my front pocket."

"Just like Mr. Smith Goes to Washington", master Craft is let loose on the world."

"Free and unshackled here I am."

The laughing and teasing continued during the 20-minute ride to the Forsythe home. Billy was introduced to Harrell's mother and sister Amy who made him feel welcomed and comfortable. He would meet Mr. Forsythe in the evening when he came from work. He carried his small suitcase to the room Mrs. Forsythe showed him. It was larger and grander than this room at home and included a private bath with a shower.

After a quick tour of the Forsythe farm which included a large barn and other buildings that held farm equipment, tools, and grain, Harrell led him to a meadow fence where they observed a herd of large cattle. Breeding a registered Angus herd was Mr. Forsythe's passion, as related by Harrell.

"Now my friend we are off to give you a new experience." Harrell offered.

"Coming from you I am afraid to guess what horror you have planned."

"I am going to introduce you to the gentleman's game of golf. When you become a congressman or governor or wealthy tycoon you will be prepared to lie to them about everything including your golf score."

"I know nothing about golf. Can I go dressed like this?"

"With me as your instructor you will be ready for the professional tour in record time and your dress is fine, shorts and short sleeved shirt, perfect."

"We will play the 9-hole course which will have fewer players to laugh at your ineptitude, but first a short lesson." As they drove the two miles to the golf club Harrel continued teasing about the prospective game.

They picked up Harrell's clubs and a bucket of balls from the clubhouse and went to the driving range.

At the driving range Harrell explained the proper grip of the golf club and the proper swing plane, then hit a few balls to demonstrate. Billy then took his turn and after several near misses he finally contacted some balls that squirted left, or right, or three feet I front of him with great consistency. After an hour and two buckets of balls, with Harrell laughing and giving instructions, he decided they were ready for their game.

"I am not near ready to play yet Harrell."

"Throwing you into the fire will temper you like a steel rod thrown into the furnace improves its quality."

"I know why you suggested this, so you could finally beat me at something."

"Yes, I will pound you like an 8-penny nail."

"What about clubs? Where will I get them?"

"We will rent them at the club house."

"Who do I pay for them?" Bill worried and wondered if the ten dollars in his pocket would be adequate.

"We will charge them to my father's account as part of his minimum."

"His minimum, what is that?"

"As a member of the club my father is required to spend a minimum amount each month either playing, eating a meal, or buying merchandise even though he may do none of those things."

"So, the club collects whether he buys or does nothing here? I should start a club like that back home, collect payment each month from people who do nothing."

"Mr. Smith's education is just beginning."

Picking up Billy's bag of clubs, Harrell had his own set, they proceeded to the first tee of the short course. There Harrell's sister Amy met them to play also.

Looking at his bag," Why are there so many clubs? There is only one ball." was Billy's smartass observation.

"Mr. Smith welcome to Washington"

Harrell hit first landing his ball several yard down the fairway. Billy waited for Amy to hit.

"She drives from the tee box out in front of us, a little shorter for the ladies."

"Then where do I hit from since I will be shorter than any of us?"

"You are a big boy Mr. Smith you hit from here same as me."

Billy swung and did make contact squirting one to the right about seventy-five yards. And the round began.

After several hits and a few misses by Billy they finished the first hole, accompanied by fits of laughter and a few hoorays from Harrell, commenting on an occasional nice shot by Billy. Amy tolerated the twosome and played better than either. By the third hole Billy was doing better and even made a few fine shots. Then Harrell hit his ball in the creek running parallel to the fairway.

"Do you have a club with water wings?" Billy laughed

"I will drop here and take a one stroke penalty." Harrell responded removing the ball from the water.

"Why?"

"Because I had an unplayable lie."

"Is that the same as a bold-faced lie? You get to place your ball in a nice place and suffer only a one stroke penalty?"

"That's the rule."

"Then I wish to place my ball up next to the hole and take my one stroke penalty."

"You would have to smarten up just to be dumb. Hit from where you lie" was Harrell's reply.

When the third hole was finally completed Amy said she was going to finish and go for a swim.

"I have enjoyed this about as long as I can stand it." She responded laughing as she headed her cart toward the clubhouse.

"You two clowns continue doing whatever it is you have been doing. I know it is not golf." She shouted as she drove away.

They continued laughing and swinging as they finished the sixth hole. As they began the seventh a large black cloud that had been forming drew their attention. They proceeded and were about mid-way on the hole when thunder rumbled in the distance.

"As long as we don't see lightening, I think we can finish." Harrell suggested. The words had barely left his mouth when both saw a lightning strike some distance away.

"Does it really make sense to stand here holding metal lightning rods?" Billy asked.

"Well said my country friend, let's head for the club house."

They were almost to the club house when the deluge engulfed them. Still laughing they rode under the sheltered entrance and conceded the round to mother nature.

That evening at dinner Billy met Mr. Forsythe. He was interested in Billy's family farm and asked questions about what they raised, how big the farm was, and the chores Billy performed there. Billy told Mr. Forsythe how impressed he was with his herd of Angus cattle. Then he told him about his father's modest five heads of Hereford heifers as a small startup. He seemed genuinely interested and made Billy feel comfortable. As they ate Amy described her golf outing with Laurel and Hardy as she put it. Telling about them having more fun ribbing each other than playing golf, like two brothers.

The next 2 days were spent swimming, (Billy had to borrow a pair of trunks from Harrell), jogging, and playing pool, another game Billy had never played. They teased and laughed their way through two games of eight ball with Harrell winning. But most of their time was spent talking about everything. Harrell said he would start to college in the fall but was not sure about a major, and Billy speculated he would start at a junior college a driving distance from home. He would try to arrange his schedule so he could work 40 hours per week and still attend classes, and he could not ignore his farm chores. Billy knew the appropriate thing to do was to invite Harrell to spend a few days with him before the summer was over. He was a little concerned about how Harrell would feel with Billy's humble surroundings as compared to what he had here, but he knew Harrell would be very comfortable and relaxed.

"So, how about spending a couple of days at my home?"

"Sure, I would like that."

"Okay, good."

"Just tell me when I will drive up there."

"Okay then, see you next Thursday. I will meet you at the high school in town and you can follow me home."

"Sounds like a plan."

Chapter Eight

"Mom, I invited Harrell up here for a couple of days, I hope that's alright with you and Dad."

"It is the right thing to do Billy. He invited you to his home."

"Mom, his family is so well off financially and they have such a big place I just worry he will be disappointed coming here. He can have my room. I will sleep in the spare, it is smaller."

"Billy, I watched how Harrell congratulated you after you had beat him in that race, how happy he was for you. I know character when I see it. No matter how nice they dress character always shines brighter. He will be fine here, and you sleep in your room. I will wash and iron new sheets for the bed in the spare and do some dusting. Harrell will be fine there I know."

"Tell Dad I will have him help me with my chores. It may be fun to watch." Laughed Billy.

On Thursday about noon Billy drove to the school parking lot. He saw a little Volkswagen Beetle sitting all alone and drove up next to the car.

"What is that? Do you get in it or put it on?" laughed Billy

"Are you laughing at my sister's little blue bug. She let me drive it up here, and do we stop at the salvage yard on the way home to drop off your rust bucket?"

"Just get in your Love Bug and try to keep up."

At home Billy introduced Harrell to his mother who welcomed him and showed him where he would be sleeping. Harrell was very polite and made several complimentary remarks about their home. He said he was looking forward to her cooking that Billy had raved about.

"Do you boys want some lunch?"

"No mom we stopped and got a burger on the way home. I must get this spoiled young man introduced to farm work. If we are going to feed him for a couple of days we need to get him hungry." Billy chided.

"Mrs. Craft when Billy talks like that I know he has a plan to humiliate me."

" Your father has a load of hay bales he wants you to store in the barn Billy." His mother reminded him.

"I know, we are off."

Their barn was a 2-story structure with the top level even with the driveway for easy access for the tractor and other equipment to drive in directly. That level had been built into a bank that joined the road and was used to store the farm equipment. At the far end of that level was the location where loose hay or bales were stored. The lower level was used as the milking shed and shelter for the cows. A 3-sided shed at the lower level had been constructed using the barn as the back wall and was shelter for the cattle in bad weather.

Upon reaching the barn Billy explained the process. Harrell would carry the hay bales from the wagon attached to the tractor into the barn where Billy would stack them out of the weather.

They had been working and laughing for about half hour when Billy's dad walked up.

"You must be Billy's new farm helper." Mr. Craft smiled.

"Son you are carrying that hay bale like a man carrying a sick puppy, pick it up by the tie strings that will be easier."

"Thanks Mr. Craft, I am Harrell Forsythe." He held out his hand dropping the bale of hay.

"Billy has told us about you and the nice time he had at your home. Welcome to our home."

"Thanks again Mr. Craft."

When the hay had all been unloaded Billy told Harrell they had about an hour before his next chore.

"Now what is our next task?"

"In due time my friend, now let's go down by the creek and see if we can see any snakes." The creek ran through the bottom of the lower pasture near the country road.

"Be careful where you step walking through the pasture."

"I may not be a country boy but even I know not to step in cow shit."

The creek was narrow and shallow at that point with clear running water. Part of the stream was covered by overhanging sycamore trees and part was in the sun. They did spot two water snakes sunning themselves on sun warmed rocks and of course threw rocks that scared the snakes, unharmed, into the tall grass. Billy showed Harrell a place where the creek widened and was deeper, it was his swimming hole when he was younger.

"Did you skinny dip here?" Harrell laughed.

"As a matter of fact my friend Wayne and I did. A country bath for farm boys."

"Did you pee in the water like I used to do in the club pool. I would holler to Amy telling her. Do not go under water I would yell. I enjoyed hearing her scream."

"We had the natural flow of the stream to keep us clear of the pollutant unlike you piss loving city boys." This as they laughed their way back toward the house.

"Now one more job before dinner." Billy said as they made their way back to the barn.

"Stand over here by the gate and watch our assistants coming to do their part. They know what time it is."

"By our assistants I assume you mean the two cows walking this way. They do seem to know we are waiting for them."

"When I open the gate here Bessie and Mable will walk into the milking station. Then I will show you the magic of where your milk comes from. I will give them some grain to keep them contented while we milk."

"We?"

"We now have an electric milking machine." Billy explained while washing the machine and the cow's utters. He then placed the milker on Bessie.

"How much milk will you get from that one?"

"About 3 gallons plus or minus, we sell what we don't need to a wholesaler who picks up the excess supply regularly."

After a few minutes Billy switched the milker to the other cow.

"Now I have to strip." As he sat with a clean bucket beneath Bessie.

"What do you mean strip?"

"The milker doesn't get all of the milk so I will finish by hand," and proceeded to show Harrell.

"I will get about another quart by stripping. You will strip Mable."

"I am sure it will be an experience that will live long in my memory."

After the milker was removed from Mable Billy positioned Harrell in the milking position for her.

"Now one teat in each hand just squeeze and pull down."

Harrell worked at it while Billy just stood and laughed. "This is for the humiliation you gave me playing golf and pool."

"I am only getting a few drops." Harrell complained just as Mable swung her tail and hit him in the side of his head.

Billy was convulsed. "Even Mable knows you have no idea what you are doing. I wish I had a movie camera to send the film to your golf club." Harrell finally finished after some more instructions from Billy.

"Are we done here now?"

"All done Corncob, let's wash up for dinner."

Two more days and then it was time for Harrell to leave. He thanked Mrs. Craft for her hospitality who had fixed him 2 homemade cinnamon rolls and a bottle of soda for his drive home. Then he went to find Mr. Craft in the barn to thank him. Billy walked him to his bug and after a handshake and a hug and a promise to stay in touch he was off. Neither suspected nor could even imagine that it would be years before they saw each other again.

Chapter Nine

Billy worked full time at the supermarket all summer and continued to help at the farm. He had saved enough money to pay tuition at the junior college. He also planned to continue work at the supermarket on a schedule determined by his class alignment. He was not sure about a college major but took courses that would point toward a BS degree someday. He learned that his friends Wayne and Jack would attend there also, and they would all commute, taking turns driving. When their class schedules were set they got together to work out the driving schedule.

The community college only had an enrollment of about two thousand students and all either lived off campus or commuted. The college was set in a small town and supplied most of the town's people with employment either as teachers, assistants, or in some capacity supporting the school's physical plant. The curriculum was limited but did provide the basic courses that are required in most 4-year schools. They did not offer football but did offer a basketball and track program. Completing 2 years would earn a student an AA (associate) degree. Billy's plan was to earn the AA degree in hopes of one day transferring his credits to a 4-year school.

"Jack, how is the hamstring doing? I have not seen you since school was out."

"It is fine now. It took some rehabbing but feels good now. I plan to go out for track at the college. Why don't you come with me and try out?"

"Tempting Jack but my schedule is too full. You should have tried for a scholarship you were our best runner before you got hurt."

"I looked into it but they don't offer scholarship for track here."

"How about you Wayne for cross country?"

"Yea maybe. I am going to talk to the coach first."

* * * * *

Following their joint visits over the summer Billy and Harrell stayed in touch by phone every 2 or 3weeks. But when Billy began class at the junior college and Harrell enrolled at Vanderbilt University their contacts became less frequent. As always life intrudes, and the issues of the day take president. Harrell was not yet decided on a major as he told Billy. His father now wanted him to follow him into law, but Harrell felt it would be too dull for his taste.

Billy juggled his school, work at the supermarket, farm schedule and finished the first semester. He did well academically but was so worn out he worried he would not be able to continue the pace.

He was in the second week of his second semester schedule when he was handed a note during class to call home, a message that one does not wants to get in the middle of his day. He hurried to find a phone and called home. His uncle Roy answered which only added to his concern. His uncle told him his father had fallen off a ladder and broken his hip and was in the hospital. Now he hurried to find either Wayne or Jack to tell them. He had driven that day and thus Wayne and Jack would have to find another ride home. He found Wayne in the student union and told him he was driving to the hospital. Wayne told him to go. He would tell Jack and they would have one of their parents come for them.

At the hospital Billy found his mother who told him his father was resting and had been x-rayed to confirm he had a broken hip. They had given him a sedative and he was asleep. He knew his father would be more concerned about the farm and less about his condition when he awoke. Again, life intrudes and the path changes once again. It did not take Billy long to determine what he would do.

His father would be in for a long rehab. Billy would delay his schooling and would now run the farm with help from Fred the part time worker they had previously hired. He discussed this with his mother, and both went to tell his father of his plan. It did relieve his father of some of his worry but felt Billy was giving up too much. It was settled he would become average Billy Craft farmer, a long ago concern he had thought of with dread. When his father came home Billy would set with him each morning to discuss what needed to be done to keep the farm operational. And so life as a full-time farmer began.

He worked the farm all winter even though his father became able to walk. His dad was occasionally with him outside but was limited to tasks that did not require climbing or heavy lifting. Yearly maintenance on the farm tractor and other machinery was one thing his father was able to continue. Billy knew that made him feel good, that he was contributing. Luckily work on the farm in the winter was easier with no hay to harvest or plants to sow or harvest. There was still the cattle to feed and care for and the milking was a daily task. Billy had begun thinking of how he could continue to help his family and still pursue a path of his own. He had gone over the plan in his head for several days playing the part of his parents in the argument he knew would result. One evening at dinner he had a conversation with his mother and father.

"Mom, Dad I have been thinking of what I want to do."

"What do you have in mind Billy?" his mother asked.

"Now hear me out before you stop me. Dad can get round some now and Frank can do all the heavy work with Dad's supervision, I am going to join the army." He waited for the protests that were sure to come.

"Why in the world would you decide to do that." His father almost yelled.

"Billy that seems like a drastic step." His mother added

"In the army I can make more than I get working at the supermarket and I can send you all money each month. With that you can hire Frank full time. With dad supervising Frank can do all I have been doing and most of it better. Also the army will pay for my college education when I get out. I have investigated it and it is something I want to do."

So, Billy Craft would join the army.

Chapter Ten

Most of those that joined with him were 18- to 22-year-olds; a few were older. Most joined because they could not find meaningful work. As always some joined for the adventure. Some joined to fight for their country remembering family and relatives who had been lost during World War II. About 10 percent were women. A few of the men he became acquainted with in his platoon had some college, most did not. During the signup period he had arranged for a portion of his pay to be sent automatically to his family. That was very satisfying to him, besides with the Army feeding him and clothing him he had little need for money, though he did retain enough pocket money for personal things.

During basic training Billy was to learn that time management was paramount. There was so much time allotted to do each task or drill, starting with getting up, getting dressed and arriving in formation. Being late by 5 seconds guarantied some form of physical punishment. Billy had always had to juggle time before so that was not a hardship. His conditioning before joining was a help, particularly on the long hikes and formation marching. It was one day at a time. He did not try to anticipate what was next, it was seldom what you thought.

The platoon graduated in 14 weeks and were to be assigned for further training based on aptitude and proficiency. Since he had some college he was assigned to the intelligence unit. That required a special clearance and while his clearance was being reviewed for approval he was assigned to a class dealing with fundamental math, electronics, and digital theory. He was transferred to another army base for that training. That series of classes would last 4 weeks. Now that basic training was over he had more time. He wrote regularly to his parents. His mother always wrote back worrying if he had enough money for himself. He was not a big partying soldier, so his pay lasted him between the bi-weekly pay periods. He would occasionally go to the enlisted club on base with friends for a beer, his first beer was in the Army. He occasionally thought about Harrell and the good times they had but he had no way to contact him, sure that he was fully engrossed in his studies at college.

Before his next assignment he had a 10-day furlough and went home. He was anxious to see his parents and his home; he was especially looking forward to his mother's cooking. He looked forward to tasks that he previously used to dread. Wolley followed him everywhere and even Liza and Lilly remembered him. He helped Frank repair a section of the barn roof that had been leaking. His mother told him she saw his dad one day with a ladder and was going to repair the barn roof. She said she had to grab the ladder and force him to stop. She told Billy fixing that barn roof would permit his dad to quit agonizing over that, but he would find something on the farm to fret about. At mealtimes he told his mom and dad about the training saying he would soon have a permanent assignment. The 10 days flew by, though he did find time to spend an evening with Jack and Wayne. They were still in college and Jack was the premier miler on the track team. Wayne was through with cross country and those murderous hills.

The assignment to the intelligence school required being transferred to still another base. That series of studies lasted 7 months and included learning about crypto machines, how they worked and how to repair them. After graduation he went to an assignment depot and waited for his assignment. In less than a week he was shipped to Germany at an army base as a member the G2 staff. Part of the orientation there, because of their work classification, was to be incredibly careful about making friends with civilians. The daily work was routine except when he might be called in at any time of the night to help with a repair or assist with a message. There was also routine night duty on a rotating basis where he sat and watched the message machine traffic.

He became friends with Jake Wright who worked next to him. Jake had been there a year and knew the routine. Jake also knew all the places in town to frequent; the places to visit and sight see. He had a favorite café that served the traditional excellent German beer and introduced Billy to the place where they ate German Strudel and drink dark beer. That changed his life forever.

On that first visit their server was a young German girl whose name tag read Mariel. She smiled and took their order. He was smitten and could not stop looking at her as she served others. Mariel was a beautiful blonde with a perfect figure. She was about five foot five at a 115 pounds, a beautiful young German girl of about 18 or 19 years of age. Her smile had Billy mesmerized.

"Earth to Bill, earth to Bill, come in Bill." Billy had become Bill to Jake.

"Oh, wow she is one beautiful girl."

"Be careful, you know the rules."

"Let's order another round."

"You are one-beer Craft, if you drink 2 I will have to carry you back."

"Shut up, I am ordering another round," another round and another nice smile from Mariel.

Finishing the second beer Billy said, "I will order another and just nurse it along I am already feeling a little lightheaded."

"You are not such a nerd. Get you a little greased and you are just like all GIs. Ready for some action"

"My intentions with Mariel are strictly honorable. I am going to marry her one day."

"Whoa wild man, slow down."

Billy nursed his beer along reluctant to call it a night.

"Be sure to leave a big tip." was Billy's response. With one final look at Muriel, they left.

The following week went too slowly for Billy. He did not know if he would get another pass for the upcoming weekend. As it turned out he had duty that weekend so a trip to the café would have to wait another week. Mariel was all he could think about.

The following week he could not wait to get off base and headed for the café. He did not invite Jake to come with him. When he entered the café he stopped and waited inside. He wanted to see which area Mariel was serving. He waited for several minutes looking for her. Maybe she was in the kitchen, so he took a booth and sat down, still looking for her. Finally, when a girl named Elsa came to wait on him he asked if Mariel was here. She shook her head and said no. He was beyond despondent. He ordered and drank one beer, then left and returned to base. Had she quit working there? Maybe she had the day off or maybe she was home sick. Maybe he would never see her again.

All week while on duty he thought of all the possible reasons she was not working that day. On Thursday he got an 8-hour pass and went to town. Again, he entered the café and looked for her. She was nowhere to be seen. After several minutes he left without ordering.

About 10 days later with the weekend coming Jake suggested they rent a car and tour the country looking at old Bavarian castles and other points of interest.

"Sounds like a good idea Jake. We can stay intown Saturday and tour on Sunday."

"I know. You want to visit your future wife again on Saturday." laughed Jake.

"I don't think she works there anymore." He told Jake about looking for her last week.

"Cheer up my friend we will just ask one of the other servers where she lives."

"Really. Do you think they would tell me?"

"No, I was just trying to make you feel better. Chances are they would not know or reveal where to you."

"But we could ask right?"

"We can ask."

They rented the car and drove to the café. They entered and Billy dreaded what he would find out. Looking carefully, he almost shouted to Jake.

"She is here."

"I can see. Look for her serving area."

Finding a table in her area Billy was as nervous as he had ever been. What should he say to her? What is the right approach? She approached their table smiling and Billy just blurted everything out.

"Hello Mariel. My name is Billy Craft. I noticed you were not here the last two times I was here. I hope you were not sick." Now he sat looking like the idiot he sounded. Jake just sat with open mouth.

"Thank you Billy Craft. I was not sick." Her smile said she was not offended.

"This is my friend Jake." He offered awkwardly.

"Mariel, Bill and I are going to take a car ride tomorrow to look at some old castles and other sites. We could use a guide to point out places of interest." *Jake you are an absolute genius,* Billy thought.

"The area around here is quite beautiful. You boys will enjoy that I think."

"We would pay you to be our guide." *How does he think so fast?*

"No, I would never take pay to look at beauty. I will ask my friend Else if she would join us. If she says yes I will agree also." Mariel walked away to find Else.

"Jake, I could kiss you on the lips, quick thinking my man. How did you think of that so quickly? Did you notice, her English is perfect, better than ours."

"I just saw your little puppy-dog eyes looking at her, and I knew if I didn't act you would do something stupid like proposing marriage." laughed Jake.

"Thanks. I owe you."

As they ate the sandwich they had ordered and drank their beer they waited for Mariel to return with her answer. Billy mentally crossed his fingers, his legs, and his toes hoping for a positive response. Finally.

When Mariel returned she was smiling. "Else said we can meet you tomorrow in the square by the fountain for a drive through the nearby country." She said upon returning. "Tomorrow is Sunday and we do not work."

"Thank you, Mariel. We will meet you about noon if that is okay." Billy stammered a little too quickly.

"Until then. Can I serve you anything else?"

"No thank you, we are okay."

They walked out to do some window shopping and to kill some time. Billy knew he would not sleep all night. They were staying at a small hotel in town. To not be completely ignorant of the sites they may see tomorrow they picked up a brochure in the hotel and studied the historical sites nearby. Would noon tomorrow never come?

Sunday before noon they drove the rental car to the town square. Finally, noon was here and as they waited on the girls. Billy wondered. "Do you think they will show?"

As soon as he said that he saw them arriving.

Billy opened the rear door and motioned Mariel in the back and jumped in after, leaving Else the front seat with Jake. A maneuver he had practiced mentally all night.

The girls began to point out items of interest as they drove; Billy had tuned out the descriptions. He found out Mariel was nineteen and her last name was Vanderhoeven, her father was Dutch and her mother German. She was to start her third year of college in the fall. She was a science major and wanted to go into the medical field one day. He inquired about her family, her friends what she did for entertainment. He already knew her eye color blue, her hair color blonde, and she was about 5ft 4 inches tall and about 115 pounds. After a while he felt she was tired of his questions, so he began to pay attention to the drive and scenery. Sitting beside her the rest of the drive was all he wanted to do.

At the end of the day when he asked Mariel if he could see her again, she said yes. The return to the base was the happiest he had ever been, and he thanked Jake for making it all possible.

Whenever he could get a pass he would meet Mariel either after work or on the weekends, mostly Sundays. They walked, they talked, they compared areas of common interest and they always laughed.

About once every 6 or7 days Billy had night duty. The job was to sit for 8 hours in front of a decryption machine and wait for any messages. Normally the eight hours was spent reading or in Billy's case studying. He had been taking courses from a US university that had set up a program in Europe. It was good time to catch up on the homework fortified by many cups of coffee. One night he received a decrypted message which he acknowledged then carried it to the duty officer. He could not help but read what it said. A group of intelligence officers from the US was coming to investigate an intelligence breach.

The following day the head of G2 Major Hawkins assembled the intelligence group for a meeting.

"We have been alerted that there may have been a security breach here." Major Hawkins began.

"I do not know the extent of the breach or how it was discovered. I do not know who breached security or who reported it. I have been informed that a security team from the US will be here by Wednesday. I do not know if they are Military Intelligence, CIA, or FBI. I only know they will debrief and interrogate each one of us. We will be confined to base during this period, no passes. I do not know the questions they will ask but it is sure to include what you do and where you go when you are on pass. They may require a polygraph test. I just do not know. I assume they will want to know the names of any civilians with which you have been in contact. That is all I know, dismissed."

Billy's head was reeling. He would have to talk about his relationship with Mariel. Would they investigate her? His weekend pass would be cancelled, and he and Mariel had planned to attend a musical concert. He had no way of telling her he could not come. She would wonder if he had stood her up. He did not want that. He needed some way to tell her he could not come. He thought of a guy he knew in the logistic group who often travelled to the civilian airport to pick up items sent by a dependent or family friend to one of the soldiers. Maybe he could deliver a note or letter to Mariel.

He sat and composed a letter to her. In it he would only say that because of a base exercise he would not be able to get a pass for an indefinite period. He wanted to be with her and would just as soon as he was able. He told her he loved her. It was the first time he had said that to her. He hoped she believed that. Finding his acquaintance, Art Corjay, in the motor pool area, he asked him to deliver the letter to Mariel at the cafe. He did not provide details to Art the reason, only saying he could not get away himself. Art said he had a scheduled pickup tomorrow and would drop it by the café that Billy told him about.

He sought out Jake after the Major's briefing. "I will have to tell them about going out with Mariel. Do you think they will investigate and question her?"

"They almost certainly will investigate her and her family, but it will be discreet, and Mariel may never know about it." Jake offered.

"Do you think the investigators will look upon Mariel as some sort of spy?"

"Have you ever talked to her about your work on base?"

"All I have told her is that I do clerical work. I am having Art Corjay in the motor pool pass her a note saying that I am not able to see her for some period."

"That is not going to look good man. What if the investigators find out you sent a message in writing to her? It may look suspicious."

"Wow that does scare me. I hope I do not get her or her family in any trouble. I will just tell the truth to the investigative team. I have done nothing illegal."

Suddenly after about two and a half weeks the investigators were gone, no explanation. Rumors circulated that a civilian clerk who worked in the duty officer's facility had been arrested, with no explanation of what she had done.

Major Hawkins called in several of the troops individually to impart any precautions left for them by the investigators. Billy was called in and Major Hawkins told him he was to have no further contact with Ms. Vanderhoeven or her family. He was stunned.

"Why? Did they say why I cannot see her?"

"No, just that any further contact could result in disciplinary action."

"But Major I plan to marry her. There must be something you can do to find out why this restriction."

"Sorry sergeant they did not provide me with any details, just what I have told you."

"Can I go to the JAG and ask them to help me or get some advice?"

"I am not sure JAG provides legal support for an individual's personal issues."

Billy was devastated. He could not even contact Mariel to tell her of what he considered to be a big mistake by the Army. Why would the Army restrict his contact with her or her family? He had never told Mariel of his work and she had never asked anything that would make him suspicious. The next few days were torture. He could not sleep or concentrate on his work; most of all he wondered about what Mariel must be thinking.

When he talked to Jake about his dilemma he asked. "What can I do?"

"I do not know man. See the Chaplain. He can give you some advice or comfort."

"Yea maybe I will, but comfort is not what I need. It cannot hurt to see him I guess."

He decided to see the Chaplain a Lt. Col named Father Wilson and requested a meeting. After waiting two agonizing days he was summoned to the chaplain's office. He told the chaplain his story from the beginning emphasizing he had never discussed his work with Mariel.

"Sergeant Craft I sympathize with your position but the gap between chaplain and military intelligence is a wide chasm that I have never had to explore."

"Can't you even ask them through some channel or other why they think the Vanderhoeven family is an intelligence risk?"

"I am not sure I can help you sergeant but give me some time to think about this whole issue."

"Thank you sir. Should I check back with you in a day or two?"

"I will contact you sergeant."

Time passed slowly for Billy as he waited to hear from Chaplain Wilson. After a week he was frantic. Did the delay mean the chaplain had forgotten or given up, or does the delay mean he is making some progress? Finally, after about 10 days the chaplain summoned him to his office.

"Sergeant Craft through a series of my contacts who used their contacts and so on, the head chaplain of the army, my boss, was able to read the intelligence report. The report said Mariel's uncle, her father's older brother, had been a soldier at one of the Nazis concentration camps. Though that man is no longer alive, for many forgiveness comes slowly."

"So, Mariel and her family are tarnished by the same brush that painted her uncle?"

"I am afraid so. I need to investigate further about the uncle's duties at the concentration camp."

"Maybe we can do something?" Billy asked.

"I don't know sergeant, but I will let you know."

Lt. Col Wilson learned through his research that the uncle had been a low-level clerk at the concentration camp. Through his contacts he got the prohibition against Mariel's family lifted. He informed Major Hawkins who lifted the ban on Billy's access to the Vanderhoeven family.

Going to the Chaplain's office he said "Chaplin I am forever grateful for all you have done. I have one more favor if I can ask. Would you go with me to their home and help explain this whole thing?" He knew he was pushing his luck.

"Sergeant this is a little out of my wheelhouse, but I can tell the family that none of this was your doing."

"Thank you sir."

The next weekend the Chaplin and Billy went on Sunday after church to the Vanderhoeven home. The Chaplin knocked and stood at the door identifying himself explained the circumstances and apologized for any embarrassment to the family. Billy stood several paces back at the top of the porch steps. Mariel helped her father understand the Chaplin's message.

"They understand now but not sure all is forgiven. It is something they have had to deal with in the past." This was the chaplain's message as they drove back to the base.

Finally, Billy got a pass for the weekend and hurried to the café to see Mariel. She was not there. When he asked about her they said she was not at work. Since he knew where she lived, having walked her home several times, he went to her home and knocked on the front door.

Her father came to the door and Billy asked if Mariel was home.

"No."

"I just want to talk to her for a minute."

"Go away."

He left the porch, head bowed and walked down the stairs to the sidewalk. Now no one could help him.

"Bill" he turned and saw Mariel standing on the porch with folded arms.

"Mariel I just wanted to tell you I am now able to get a pass and I want to see you. Your father still seems angry."

"Bill, just leave. I will talk to my father. Come next Saturday to the café. We can talk then"

All week he worried about her father's anger. Was he forbidding her to see him? Were they interviewed during the security check, or accused of Nazi sympathies? Is that what made her father angry?

They met after her work the next Saturday and Mariel told him of her father's anger. Their friends and neighbors had been interviewed about her family and those at her work had been interviewed about her. Her father said, "Do they think we are spies because my daughter talks to a soldier? We were never Nazis." He was quite angry, and Mariel was upset as well. Billy explained without any specifics saying it was just army routine investigation.

"You will come to my home for dinner tomorrow. I have talked to my father and mother."

"Is it safe? He was so angry"

"Bring him a bottle of brandy. You and he will drink brandy and talk."

"Okay what shall I bring your mother?"

"Bring her flowers for the table. And for me, bring you."

Standing awkwardly at the front door on Sunday Billy was just short of terrified when Mariel invited him in and introduced him to her parents. If he was awkward before, standing looking at her father sitting in the parlor he created a new definition of the word. After the introductions and the gifts were offered the father opened and shared the brandy. The conversation began slowly but the brandy had a convivial affect and soon Billy was telling of his home and family. The conversation ended when they were called to the dinner table, deccorated by a beautiful vase of flowers. And the routine began, Saturday was a date with Mariel, when he could get a pass, and then Sunday dinner at the Vanderhoeven home where brandy was served first.

Chapter Eleven

Two more weeks and his tour in Germany would be over. He would be going home, he and Mariel. The wedding had been a month ago in Mariel's church. It was a small wedding, just her mother and father, two aunts and uncles, and four of Mariel girlfriends. Jake and Chaplin Wilson were his only attendants and Jake was his best man. The Chaplin read their vows. While Billy finished things on the base, Mariel was home packing boxes that would be sent when they had a mailing address in the states.

He would have 30 days leave when they got to the US; they would first visit his parents. He had written them about Mariel, the wedding, and how happy he was, His mother was so excited to meet Mariel and of course Billy as well. He knew his mother would want to spend hours talking to her about her home, her wedding, her family, and a thousand other things.

* * * * *

When they arrived in the US Billy had to check into his base at a post in Virginia. He had put Mariel in a motel nearby and told her he would be back soon with his leave papers. He hurried back in 4 hours knowing she would be nervous staying there alone. They rented a car and opted for good night's sleep before heading to his home early in the morning.

On the drive he kept up a constant description of his farm, his friends, the countryside, and answering anything she wanted to ask. Driving up the old gravel road to the farm he suddenly realized how much he had missed it all. When they pulled up beside the house they had not even got the car doors open until his mother came running arms outstretched, his father followed behind. He got a quick hug and a kiss before she grabbed Mariel crying with joy.

"My son and daughter are home at last." she sobbed still holding on to Mariel.

He got a hug and handshake from his father who exclaimed. "She is beautiful Billy.

"Tell her dad, not me. I already know." Billy was laughing with tears in his eyes.

"Both of you come in here and eat I know you must be starved."

"We ate on the way mom."

"Nonsense that was not home cooking. I must show Mariel what I have made. You will both eat some more."

His dad produced a couple of beers which surprised Billy. They watched his mother explain to Mariel how she prepared certain items while Mariel asked questions and was interested in all Mrs. Craft told her. During the evening Billy did not believe his mother was more than two feet away from Mariel the whole time. She must have hugged Mariel 15 times before we all went to bed. The next morning Billy was anxious to show Mariel around the farm describing all the things he had to do growing up. Wolley followed them everywhere. When Mariel noticed they had chickens she told Billy about raising chickens at her home.

"I am sure when my mother hears that she will invite you to go with her for eggs."

"I love your mother, and your father too. They make me less homesick."

"I promised your father when we got settled and have our own place, we would come to visit them once a year."

"I know, he made me promise to keep reminding you." Mariel laughed

Mrs. Craft game out heading to the chicken house.

"Mrs. Craft I will go with you and see your chickens."

"Well bless you dear, come along. You can call me Jenny, or even mom if you want instead of Mrs. Craft."

"For now it will be Jenny, alright."

"Don't take too long we have a chore to do before dinner." Billy called after them

"A chore, what? Mariel puzzled.

"Surprise."

His mother and Mariel fed the chickens, gathered the eggs, and then picked some green beans for dinner. They talked the whole time. About 4 o'clock Billy took Mariel out to the barn and stood by the gate to the pasture.

"What is our chore here?"

"We must wait, they will be along soon."

"Who will be along soon?"

"The cows."

"Don't you have to go round them up like cowboys?" She laughed."

"No, they will come on their own. They know I am home and will want to see me." he teased.

The two cows ambled up the meadow Billy opened the gate and the cows just walked by and went into the barn to the milking station. Mariel watched in surprise.

"See I told you, they wanted to see me."

Billy applied the milking machine to one cow he called Bessie.

"This is Bessie, the other is Mable."

She watched as he went about the whole process. He told her about his friend Harrell and how he laughed when Harrell tried to hand milk Mable and how Mable had hit him in the head with her tail.

"You really enjoy the farm, don't you?" Mariel queried.

"I do or did. It is all I knew growing up."

"We should buy a farm someday." She suggested

"Maybe babe, but that is a long way off."

Chapter Twelve

With his parents blessing Harrell enrolled at Vanderbilt in the fall following high school graduation. He had not settled on a major knowing the first-year curriculum would be about the same for every major. Also, he was not ready to decide. His father said college would give him maturity and improve his outlook on life by being exposed to the diversity of other students and professors. His grandfather said" do not just observe life, participate" and Harrell did.

Because of his success in high school the Vanderbilt track coach sent a letter suggesting he show up for track in the spring, but he was undecided about doing so. Early on the fraternities were having rush week and more out of curiosity than interest he attended some fraternity parties. The beer there was plentiful, and he imbibed finding out that drinking was something at which he was not particularly good. Two beers made him woozy and a third had him on his knees with his head in a toilet. Surviving that he did enjoy the friendship and eventually he joined the Phi Kaps.

After thinking it over he did apply to the track team. In high school he was so naturally talented that he did not have to work hard to be better than those around him. He found college track practice was much different. These guys worked hard each day and he was always behind in the routine. He still had the drive he always had and soon he became at least competitive. In the first two meets he did not qualify to be one of Vanderbilt's milers. He was not used to being second best at anything and began to work harder and eat a proper diet. Finally, he became the third best miler on the team and ran in the next meet, coming in fourth in the meet against Tennessee. The coach approached him and told him he had a future as a miler during his next 3 years. He was supposed to feel good about the compliment, but waiting was not his forte.

He was determined to be good enough to be a winner as a freshman. He decided his sprints needed to improve. One day in the sprints he decided to best all the runners and suddenly pulled away from them. He was trying harder than he had ever run. But the pace devised by his brain was an over match for his muscles and he suddenly went down in pain. It was a pulled hamstring he knew, and that was soon confirmed by the trainer. The trainer told him it would be weeks before he could even run and track for this year was over, rest was the only therapy. As he limped around attending class he knew his boyhood dream of running in the Olympics was now over. He wondered often if Billy was somewhere running with Olympic dreams still intact. He called Billy at home once only to find he was away in the army.

Beginning his sophomore year he was still not settled on a career path but that changed one day at a fraternity party when he caught site of Lisa Ann Holdren. Lisa Ann was outgoing, smart, and a dark-haired beauty. He made it a priority to get to know her. He found out she was a premedical student and planned to be a family doctor. She had come from a small town in Tennessee and planned to return to practice there when she became a doctor. She was the classic high school over achiever graduating as valedictorian. College had always been her dream but it hit a sudden bump when her father died when she was a senior. Now she felt she needed to stay home and help her mother. Her older brother by 3 years was already out his own doing carpenter work and was engaged to be married. Her mother worked in city hall and with her father's insurance she assured Lisa Ann she was ok financially. Her home was paid for and insisted Lisa Ann proceed with her college plans of becoming a doctor. Lisa Ann had scholarships from organizations in town and her mother convinced her to go. She enrolled at Vanderbilt that fall and was excited to begin her career.

When Harrell learned she planned to go to medical school his die was also cast. If she wanted to be a doctor, then he wanted to be a doctor. If she had wanted to be a geologist, he would have hunted rocks with her. Sometimes life turns on such seminal moments.

Thus began their relationship. He would make premed his major also. It was not long until they were remarkably close and spent all their time together either studying or just enjoying all that life had to offer.

He never returned to the track team. He did join the ROTC. He had always been patriotic and decided if his country needed him he would serve. He returned home for holidays at Thanksgiving and Christmas and also in the summer to work on the farm, or ranch as it was becoming. He called Billy's home one summer to get his army address, only to find out he was in transit and had no permanent address.

When he and Lisa Ann were admitted to med school Harrell found the studies there were a challenge, but a challenge is what always inspired him just like when he ran track, always wanting to be first. In the third year of med school they got married, this against the advice of her mother and brother. Harrell's parents, being well off financially, bought them an apartment for their wedding present and they settled in there to finish school.

"looking at your high school yearbook I see you said you always wanted to be a doctor." Harrell commented one evening during a relaxing period as he thumbed through her yearbook.

"Yes, I did. What did you aspire to be?"

"A winner in the Olympic mile run."

"Obviously you can close that fairy-tell book, what next?"

"When we become doctors I think we should move to Bora Bora and practice there."

"Bora Bora? We would not be licensed to practice there."

"We will be witch doctors, live in a grass hut near the beach, and tend to the local natives."

"Harrell, I think all this studying has flipped your brain. How would we live? What would we eat?"

"The natives will bring us small pigs and coconuts for our service."

"I would never trust you treating all of those lithe attractive young native girls."

"And I would worry about you treating those bronze young bodies every day. I would have you wear a chastity belt, and I will keep the key on a string around my neck."

"Those bronze young bodies do sound interesting. Around MY neck I would have a very sharp knife on a string and if you got too friendly with the sweet young things I would help you learn to sing a few octaves higher."

"Really, you are not a surgeon."

"True, but I know anatomy and where all the parts are."

"Then I guess I could throw away that key and join the ladies choral group."

"Enough of your wild imagination swings now get back to Gray's Anatomy."

"I will learn my anatomy in braille. You know, first-hand knowledge, with you as my subject."

To relieve the grueling study routine Harrel often digressed into these fits of wild imagination. He often told Lisa Ann about his friend Billy Craft, about running against each other in track, and about all the fun they had when together. He also wondered what had happened to Billy, but there was never enough time to try to find out. Life gets hold of our lives and carries us forward in a seemingly predetermined path.

When Harrell's father died he left Harrell and his sister Amy the farm and a significant sum of cash (mostly in bonds). Amy said she preferred to keep the farm and live in the house with their mother. This was with Harrell's complete agreement. Amy and her husband were well qualified to run the farm. She would keep part of the cash to help run the farm and the remaining cash and bonds would be Harrell's. They both felt comfortable with this agreement.

Harrell had just completed his third year of medical school when he received a phone call from Lt Col Gray, the commandant of the ROTC on campus. He asked Harrell to come by and see him. What can this be about he wondered telling Lisa Ann about the call.

"You are no longer in ROTC. That ended with your undergraduate work didn't it?" She asked.

"Yes. I do have an option to join the army reserves after medical school, but it is much too soon to think about that." I will go by tomorrow and see what he wants."

During the lunch period the following day Harrell knocked on the door of the Lt. Col. "Come in Mr. Forsythe." The colonel offered his hand smiling.

"Good day sir. I cannot imagine why you wanted to see me."

"I have a suggestion, a request actually. We are extremely short of army doctors at all our US army hospital facilities. Many have been transferred away to support our troops in southeast Asia. Places like Walter Reed and other army hospitals are spread very thin of doctors. Would you consider a brief appointment, after graduation, to work at one of these hospitals to give the army medical staff some much needed help."

"Wow I never saw that coming. I do not know what to say. I must think about that and discuss it with my wife. It would be a major shift in our plans. How long a period are we talking?"

"I cannot say for certain but perhaps a 2-year appointment. I believe you would be given the rank of captain for that period. I thought the captain's salary could create a small nest egg for you before establishing your own practice. There would also be the added benefit of having access and experience using the latest medical and surgical equipment. It would just be a continuation of your internship."

"Colonel at present I am overwhelmed. How soon do you need a decision?"

"If you could let me know within two weeks I would appreciate it. If your answer is yes I can get the ball rolling, if it is no then I need to consider other avenues."

"I will let you know after discussing it with my wife."

As he walked from the Colonel's office toward their apartment he was thinking about what Lisa Ann would think. Out of patriotism he wanted to say yes to the suggestion but that was not fair to Lisa and the plans they had mapped out. Their plan was to set up a joint family practice in Lisa's hometown. She had received scholarship help from organizations in town and felt the need to honor the community that helped her. Maybe she would talk him out of the colonel's request. Knowing her as he did he knew she would listen to his desires, and he wasn't sure what was the proper thing to do.

Chapter Thirteen

Bill was assigned to an army base near Washington D.C. to finish out his tour of duty. He and Mariel settled into an efficiency apartment nearby. In a few months he would have to be thinking about his work after discharge. He stayed in contact with his mother and father via frequent phone calls and letters back and forth. His mother had been telling them about the failing health of his father. She asked Billy's help in convincing his father about selling the farm. He was no longer able to work. He knew that would be devastating to his father. The farm had been his life for 80 years. He was born there. Billy called his uncle Roy and aunt Peggy to ask their opinion and to solicit their help talking to his father. Billy took a long weekend and he and Mariel drove to the farm to address the inevitable.

"I know why you are here. You want us to sell the farm. Your mother believes we should, and I know she has been talking to you and to Roy about it." George said.

"What do you want to do dad?"

"What I want to do is go mow the upper pasture and get the beef cattle ready for market. That is what I want to do, but that ship has sailed for me. What I must do is sell the farm and quit growling at your mother for asking me to take it easy."

The rest of the stay that weekend was planning the operation that would proceed. It was agreed they would sell the farm in its entirety, land, equipment, livestock. They would keep the house and a small vegetable garden behind the house. Uncle Roy would help with the process. Billy and Mariel left after the weekend relieved that his father had agreed, but it was one of the saddest days Billy could remember.

"Mariel, I have a feeling this is the beginning of the end for dad. His health has not been good and giving up the farm will hasten his end, I fear. He really agreed to the sale for mom's sake. The tough old bird always wanted to keep mom happy."

"Bill I can go down there and help with things when they have the sale finalized." Mariel offered.

"I know my mother would appreciate your help and your company."

In a few short weeks the farm was sold, and George and Jenny settled into their new existence. Billy constantly checked with his uncle Roy about how they were all doing. It would just be a few months until his enlistment was up, and he and Mariel were thinking and planning of where to go and what do to do in their civilian life. After discharge they had decided to move to the town where the state university was located. Both could continue their education while finding work. Their life like most lives was like a meandering stream headed down toward an unknown tributary. Sometimes the stream flowed swiftly, other times it was a slow calm flow.

The last 2 years had been a whirlwind of activities for Billy. The army duty, his marriage to Mariel, the move back to the US, all seemed so long ago and yet it had gone by in a flash. From time to time he did think about Harrell and what he was doing and what he had become. He remembered the long conversations both had, discussing religion, politics, war, and life in general. Two adolescents with no experience in life and no formal education discussing these items with opinions that now made him smile. They talked of religion and fate and whether they believed in fate. Harrell brought up in a strict Catholic family atmosphere did not believe in fate. He always said God gave us free choice.

Billy would argue that the fate and free choice were not mutually exclusive. He said the many twists and turns of their lives were the result of free choice, but that there could still be a plan in place to bring us to the end fate had chosen. Harrell of course disagreed. He smiled to himself remembering those conversations. He wondered what fate had in store for him and for Harrell.

He also smiled to himself about the time he spent at Harrel's home and how Harrell had short-sheeted him and laughed at his puzzled discomfort. Billy had reciprocated when Harrel visited the Craft farm by filling his pillow with prickly straw. Harrel said he had never slept on a porcupine for a pillow. Those were good times so long ago.

Most people when they think of fate it is the crowning achievement of an individual as if preordained, or sometimes it is the tragic death of an individual in some bizarre circumstance. Harrell felt that after these events people ascribed the event as fate when their free will brought them to that point or that end. Billy felt fate was the process that an individual traverses in their life, the path that nature or God had prescribed.

"I think there must a single molecule among our body's millions of molecules that is designated the pathfinder determining our fate." Billy had suggested to Harrell.

"And just how does that molecule derive this information?" Harrell had responded.

"By chance I believe. Like the infinite monkey theory which implies all things are possible given enough opportunities. Or maybe it is the law of large numbers or something like that."

"You mean like the infinite monkeys and infinite typewriters theory?" Harrell had roared dismissing Billy's explanation. And so their many discussions went, often with divergent beliefs none of which would alter their friendship.

To Billy life was like a giant jig-saw puzzle with millions of pieces and multiple colors in which a life would unfold. Woven into that puzzle was a miniscule painted path for each person. Though circuitous there was a path for each to follow. He had read of individuals who had perished under dire circumstances while others in the same scenario had survived. He remembered Captain Eddie Rickenbacker surviving in a life raft for 24 days in the Pacific and later becoming a world renown pioneer in American aviation, while others with him perished. Maybe fate was more a feeling than an actual belief, though he could not shake the idea that it was not real.

Just 2 weeks before his discharge his uncle Roy called with news. When he heard Roy's voice he did not have to ask why, he knew. His father had died peacefully in his sleep. Aunt Peggy was with Jenny and Roy was making funeral arrangements. Billy and Mariel packed quickly and headed home.

Even when you know it is coming you put off the grief, saving it for the day when it can no longer be held in check. Then it all becomes suddenly so final and emotions are released. Having friends come to the house with food and condolences provided a level of comfort, especially for his mom. Billy could not help walking all about the farm remembering everything that happened there like it was only yesterday, the rains that prevented the hay harvest, the tractor breaking down, patching holes in the chicken house to keep out weasels and racoons. Each event came back with a clarity he had never experienced. As he stood and looked at the upper pasture he could see his grandfather slumped over on the tractor, the tractor still running but not moving. He was 10 or 11 and could see his mother running to his grandfather's side yelling for someone to call for a doctor. He could see Mr. Hazelton the milk man who picked up their milk cans regularly running up the pasture toward his mother and grandfather. He had parked his truck at the bottom of the driveway and was running toward them through the hip-deep hay that had not been mowed. The picture was as clear as a painted picture hanging on a wall. All the colors, Mr. Hazelton's black hat, his mother in a white apron, the red tractor, the green brown of the mowed hay, the green of the not yet mowed hay. The picture was only there for a minute but would be stored in his mind forever. Smiling, in his mind's eye he could still see Harrell trying to milk Mable. Or was it Bessie?

It was agreed after the funeral that his mother would go spend a few days with uncle Roy and Aunt Peggy. She just wanted to talk and talk with someone about their whole life on the farm. She said she wanted to go back to their farmhouse in a few days. She was not ready to leave that house until she had rung out all the living memories there.

Chapter Fourteen

One month after completing his final year of medical school Harrell walked into Walter Reed Medical Center in Washington DC. The discussion with Lisa Ann prompted them to form a new plan. They would still open a medical practice in Lisa Ann's hometown in northern Tennessee. The full team would not be in place until Harrell had finished the tour he had agreed to.

Initially they would rent a small efficiency apartment near Walter Reed and Lisa would stay for a while as they discussed the new plan. She would then go to her hometown and start the process of setting up a practice. She had received scholarship help from several organizations there and felt obligated to serve that community. Harrell would fly down weekends when he was free. Together they would find a place for an office and clinic. Harrel would concentrate on state licenses and insurance while Lisa would concentrate on developing the clinic.

They found a location in the middle of town that had previously been a bakery and while the space was adequate it needed much work to turn it into professional doctor's offices and clinic. It was their good fortune that Lisa's brother, Paul, was a carpenter and contractor and refurbishing homes and offices was his business. Lisa told him what she wanted and together they had an architect draw up the plans.

"Harrell, I know Paul will want to charge us only the minimal price for his work. I will insist he be paid whatever his normal rates are."

"I agree. We have the bonds left me by my father. You work out the cost of the refurbishment and I will cash the bonds we need to complete the work. Tell him if he doesn't charge us his regular rate we will get another contractor."

Harrell could only stay with Lisa 2 or 3 days when he came and then it was back to Walter Reed. His first week on the job he had followed around a captain, a senior doctor, and became his Saint Bernard trailing after him. He followed him to each ward where they saw each patient and took the time with each as was needed both medically and personal. The doctor in charge of hospital operations, a Colonel Wilson, had given him one piece of advice. "When you are talking to a patient take your time, do not rush. At that moment he is your only concern, and he needs to believe that."

After a week of trailing Captain Evert he was told he was now on his own and given his area of responsibility. The scarcity of doctors meant everyone would be busy and must work their wards with senior consultation only when necessary. Quite often it was a 12-hour shift. He was learning about wounds and diseases he had never encountered. He even pulled shifts in the OR assisting surgeons. He observed and did the closeup, stitching up incisions. After work he was too tired to do anything but call Lisa, telling her of his day and enquiring about her progress. Whenever he got off at a decent hour he would jog throughout the Walter Reed campus. Often when jogging he would be reminded of his days with Billy Craft. Remembering always made him smile. Other than his family and Lisa, Billy Craft was the only other person he had felt close to. Lisa always worried about him asking if he was eating properly and getting enough rest. He always said yes but his body at times said "no".

It was only natural to become personally acquainted with several of the men in his wards. Many had been there for months rehabbing, getting prosthetics, or just letting their wounds and minds heal. He would take to time to chat about their families and their homes. He became acquainted with two who came from the area where Lisa had setup the clinic, one from Kentucky, one from Tennessee. He told them of the clinic and about his beautiful intelligent doctor wife. He invited them to visit when they got home. The Kentucky soldier told him of his home and that most of his family worked in the coal mines and how dangerous and hard it was to work there. One day he told Harrell he was lucky he was disabled; it would save him from the mines where his father had worked for 35 years. Harrell knew it was not said in jest.

His regular flights were into Knoxville where Lisa would meet him and take him to the apartment she had rented. After one such flight as Lisa drove and talked about her progress, he went sound asleep sitting beside her. They had planned to go directly to the clinic to see Paul's progress.

"The progress on the clinic can wait; you need to go to bed and get some rest."

"Okay, let me take a short nap and then we will go." It was about 4PM when he laid down. He awoke to music from a radio and noise coming from the kitchen. It was 7:30 AM.

"Lisa, why didn't you wake me?"

"An exploding bomb would not have awakened you. You are exhausted and have lost weight. Are you eating regularly?"

"The meals in the cafeteria are fine, when I can work them into my schedule. I am so busy some days that it never even crosses my mind to eat."

"I know you are invested in your work. I know it is important to you and to those you help, but unless you want to begin our practice as a doctor and not as a patient you need to take time to stay healthy."

"I will. I am familiar with the routine now and will try to be more self-aware. What is for breakfast?"

One week he had worked a double shift twice because another doctor had been transferred. He ran into captain Frank Evert leaving his ward.

"Stop, let me look at you. You are jaundiced. Your eyes are yellow. Come with me to the lab, we need to draw some blood." Evert said.

Less than an hour later he was admitted to the officer's ward, a saline drip in his left arm. He knew he had to call Lisa and was dreading the call. He had been at Walter Reed a little more than 8 months and knew he had about another 16 months left on his tour. He needed to get to Tennessee to help Lisa and knew telling her of his situation could complicate their plans.

Once again he had interrupted their plans, first by signing up for this assignment, and now the monkey wrench of his illness. He made the call and downplayed his illness, but he was talking to a doctor and she asked all the right questions. She would be there tomorrow.

Lisa arrived as scheduled next day. She had already talked to his attending physician. He tried to talk to her about the clinic and how things were progressing.

"Let us concentrate on you getting well. The clinic is moving along. You need to rest and drink all the water they bring you each day. Right now alcohol is a out. I am sure they will be doing more blood work to further diagnose the severity."

"Babe, I know I am adding to your anxiety about the decisions I have made taking this assignment."

"Let me tell you what my mother told me years ago when I was having a problem about something or other. She said life is like a rolling landscape of hills and valleys. Each hill must be climbed, and each valley enjoyed for a short time before the next hill looms. Rarely will the forward landscape be level."

"That is just life Harrell. We just take a breather and move on."

"You never told me your mother majored in philosophy." He joked.

"She majored in common sense."

"The best guess they tell me is that I will remain here for about 5 days until the jaundice clears up. Then I will be released and told to rest for 10 days. Now go home, quit worrying about me, and I will be with you in about a week."

* * * * *

It had been almost 3 years since Harrell was discharged from Walter Reed and the army. He was discharged after serving only 16 months based on a COG (Convenience of the government) order. He had never heard of that but was overjoyed to be going home to be with Lisa.

He had jumped right into the work at their clinic with enthusiasm and joy. Lisa Ann had done a remarkable job getting everything organized and Paul had remodeled the building as requested.

They had two employees, Margaret Nestor the receptionist who had been a God send. She previously worked at the local hospital and knew the process for filing insurance forms. She filled a great need they had been worried about. The second employee was a young RN Alice Rogers. Initially she had taken the job as a temporary assignment while waiting for an appointment as a surgical nurse. Lisa Ann was in dire need at the time and agreed to her temporary assignment. Alice became so involved with all who came in, especially the recurring patients, and with Lisa that she asked if she could stay on permanently. This was met by a big hug and a loud yes from them both.

The biggest event since his discharge was the birth of their daughter Hazel Marie, now almost two and the joy of their lives. Lisa had stayed home for almost 3 months with the baby, and Harrell ran the clinic with help from another retired doctor friend. Lisa did go in on occasion when the workload demanded. After 3 months Lisa Ann returned full time and her mother Marie stayed with the baby. The baby's middle name Lisa Ann chose, with Harrell's concurrence, was to honor her mother who had sacrificed much helping Lisa Ann with her education.

At work one day Alice interrupted Harrell to tell him he had a phone call. "A Mr. Anthony Mauro asks to speak to you."

"I do not recognize the name. Did he say what he wanted?" Somehow the name sounded familiar, but he was not a recent patient.

"This is Doctor Forsythe. How can I help you?"

"You may not remember me, but I was a patient of yours at Walter Reed."

"I thought the name was familiar, now I remember. You were getting a prosthesis for a leg or an arm as I recall. Nice to hear from you Anthony, hope things are going well and you are now home."

"Yes, I am fine. It was an arm and a leg doctor."

"It is great to talk to you. Anything I can do to help you?"

"I hope so. It is about my father. He has, we believe, black lung disease and he is not getting help from doctors locally who were suggested by the mine company."

"Bring him in Anthony. We will see what we can do. My wife is also a doctor and she has seen one or two black lung cases. Maybe she can help."

"Do I need to make an appointment?"

"Just tell me when you can bring him here and we will fit him in."

"Thanks Doctor Forsythe. I will let you know."

That evening Harrell told Lisa about the phone call. He also told her about treating Anthony at Walter Reed, telling her about his prosthesis and about his father. She said there was no cure for black lung she knew about, but perhaps some medication to aid breathing and some diet and exercises that might help.

A week later Anthony called and said he would like to bring his father that day. He said it was about a 2-hour drive and they could be there about 10 or 10:30. Harrell told him to bring him right to the clinic and gave Anthony the address.

When they arrived Anthony introduced his father, Mario. Mr. Mauro was a small-boned man with sad grey eyes and a nagging cough. Anthony said he was fifty-eight but he looked to be eighty. He had worked in the coal mines since he was eighteen, it was all he knew. Harrell asked mister Mauro to wait while he got some information from Anthony.

"Did you drive down here today or did your father?" Harrell inquired looking at the two prostheses.

"Yes doctor I drove, it is only my left side, the right leg and arm are still original." He said with a small laugh.

"Tell me about your father and his condition."

"He had to stop working about a year ago. He has no insurance and just a small unemployment income. The doctors there as recommended by the mine operator refuse to confirm he has black lung caused by the mine. They say his condition is caused by his years of smoking. His smoking I agree is an aggravating factor but that did not cause all his symptoms. He does not sleep well due to his coughing, and he has lost weight over the last year."

"I want my wife to examine him. She has some experience with treating 2 or 3 former miners who have come here."

Lisa Ann did examined Mr. Mauro and gave him some medicine to aid his breathing and counseled him on his smoking. She was not an expert on black lung, but she was reasonably sure that was his main issue. She talked to Anthony, and Harrell and suggested he return in two weeks for a more thorough examination and to see if the medicine she gave him was helping his breathing.

They both talked to Anthony about the mine and whether it had adequate fresh air ventilation. They knew there had been requirements instituted by the UMW (United Mine workers) that safety and proper ventilation was the law.

"The way these mines work is that some have no union. When they try to organize the mine operators close the mines, until out of desperation and needing to work, the miners agree not to organize. When they become sick the operators send them to their doctors who prescribe some medicine and tell them to go back to work." Anthony said.

"I thought John L. Lewis and the UMW made them clean up the mines and permit them to organize."

"He did make great headway on improving mine safety but the mine inspectors, when available, are too few and are persuaded by the mine operators to be less diligent. Whenever the UMW has its head turned some mines ignore or water-down the safety requirements. There are still unsafe mines and unsafe conditions especially in the smaller mines."

"Have you thought about trying to sue the operators?"

Anthony laughed. "That takes money and lawyers who can wage years of legal wrangling. Defendants too are hard to convince for their testimony, fearing family reprisals. That is not an option for us."

"If you tell me what I owe you for the visit and medicine today I can pay. I have my total disability that I use to keep the family housed and fed. We also have chickens and hogs which we butcher each fall and that keeps us in the meat and eggs we need." Anthony added.

"There is no charge today Anthony." Harrell looked at Lisa who nodded in agreement.

"Dad will not like that. He has always told us to pay our obligations. He will want to reimburse you."

"Tell him when you butcher this fall to send us some sausage or ham and that will be adequate compensation. Also, I am going to talk to a lawyer friend of mine about what can be done to get your father full workers' compensation." Harrell said.

It was not uncommon for the clinic to be paid by the barter method. They never pressed their patients for reimbursement. Lisa wanted to repay the community for the help they gave her, and she never asked for payment when she knew a patient was having a hard time financially. They let them pay when they could and what they could. Quite often 2 dozen eggs or a newly butchered ham would be provided with only little or no explanation. Was the largesse a gift or was it partial payment of a medical bill? In hunting season it was common to receive a deer hind quarter or 2. Normally they gave that to Lisa's brother Paul.

Thanking them both and promising to bring his father back in 2 weeks he went to find his father who was outside having a smoke.

"Harrell you know they won't be able to afford a lawyer." Lisa said.

"I know. I will see if Dan Howard can do something pro bono."

Harrell's friend Dan Howard, a lawyer, was a weekend golfing friend. He would talk to him to see if anything could be done to help Mr. Mauro.

When Anthony brought his father back in 2 weeks Lisa saw he was no better. The medicine had helped his cough and he said he had slept better. All she could do was treat the symptoms. There was no cure for black lung of which she was aware.

Harrell had talked to Dan Howard who had agreed to investigate the matter pro bono. Dan asked Lisa to prepare a detailed examination report on Mr. Mauro's health. Dan also asked Harrell to get a detailed report on Mr. Mauro's history of working in the mine, how long there, the working conditions, etc. He said he might be able to use that as a tool to show the mine operators they were responsible for Mr. Mauro's health and were legally required to compensate him for his inability to work.

He told Harrell and Lisa that it was all he could do. He could not afford to get into a long legal fight with mine lawyers. He was hoping the threat of a lawsuit would motivate them to assist Mr. Mauro with his health issues and provide proper compensation, but he was not at all optimistic. He would attach Lisa's health report to a letter he would send them.

It was about 2AM about 3 months after Dan Howard had sent the letter to the mine operator when there was a loud knocking on Harrell and Lisa's front door. A police officer there told him their clinic was on fire.

Harrell slipped on pants and sweatshirt and headed to the clinic. He told Lisa to stay with Hazel Marie; he would call her later.

By the time he arrived at the clinic the fire had been extinguished. The front reception area and one of the exam rooms had been destroyed but the remaining rooms and equipment had not burned. The fire chief said the front window had been broken and an accelerant had been thrown through the widow and set on fire. He said it looked like an obvious case of arson.

He called Lisa and gave her the news. Neither could think of anyone who would want to burn down the clinic. The next day Lisa joined Harrell to get a complete evaluation of the damage. They would call Paul, Lisa's brother, and see if he could get his crew there to begin the tear-out and rebuild. As they were wondering that evening about who could have a disagreement with them and the clinic, they received a phone call from Dan Howard who told them his car had been vandalized the same night. Two windows had been broken out and two tires slashed. As they talked both arrived at the same conclusion, it was due to the letter Dan had sent to the mine operator.

There was no way to prove the mine operator was involved. Their insurance covered most of the clinic rebuild. Dan told them without a witness to the fire or some direct evidence there was no way they could bring a lawsuit. Lisa was adamant about telling the local papers about the fire and her suspicion about why it had happened. She was careful about making a direct accusation but took the opportunity to talk about black lung and those she had treated from the mines.

A week after the fire Anthony called to say his father had passed away. He had heard about the fire and had the same suspicions as they about the source. He said his father had received some pressure about going to their clinic for treatment. Anthony said he would ask around to see if he could pick up any talk about who might have ordered or caused the fire. Harrell told him to not endanger his family or himself, to just let it alone. He offered their condolences about his father's passing.

Ten days later Harrell was at the clinic, which was undergoing repairs, when called to the phone. "Doctor Forsythe this is Anthony. I have some information about the fire at the clinic."

"Do you know who was responsible?"

"I think so. Is there any way you could come up here in a few days?"

"I could drive up there Saturday I think."

"Come to my mother's house. You have the address."

It was an hour and a half to two for the drive. Lisa Ann stayed behind telling Harrell not to get in trouble there. Arriving at Anthony's mother's house Harrell could see it was a house that could stand some repair and some new paint. It looked as though Anthony had done some repair to places on the roof. Working with one good hand and one good leg Harrell wondered how he was able to climb up there and effect the repair. Anthony came to the door when Harrell knocked and invited him in.

"Come into the kitchen Doctor that's where we do all our talking here." Anthony said with a short laugh and introduced his mother who was there working. The house may have been old and outdated but it was spotlessly clean.

"Nice to meet you Mrs. Mauro. Anthony told me how he liked your cooking when he was in Walter Reed. He wanted to get home and eat some of your blackberry cobbler."

"Doctor, I want to thank you for helping my husband and Anthony."

"I am sorry we couldn't do more to help Mr. Mauro."

"I understand doctor. He waited too long and never got the proper help here. Can I get you something to eat or drink?"

"No thank you."

"Mom, I have somethings I want to talk to the Doctor about."

"I know. I am leaving but give the Doctor some of that blackberry cobbler to take home before he leaves."

"Doctor Forsythe, I want to take you to meet a lady, a Mrs. Platt. If you drive I will direct you to her place. She will only talk to us while her husband is working at the mine today.

With Anthony as a guide they drove a short distance to the Platt house which was only about a mile from the Mauro's home. It sat on a small hill with no other house close by. Her house was in a little better shape than the Mauro's. Having an able-bodied man available for repairs was obvious. Mrs. Platt came to the door and invited them in. After the introductions Anthony asked Mrs. Platt to tell the doctor what she had told him.

"Doctor, it gives me much pain to have to tell you what I know about the fire at your clinic. My husband does not know I am talking to you. I am a Christian woman and I know right from wrong. Setting fire to your clinic was wrong."

"What do you know about who set the fire Mrs. Platt?"

"My 2 oldest boys, age 18 and 20 set the fire."

"Why would they do that? Where are they now?"

"They did it to save their father's job at the mine."

"I don't understand?"

"Several days ago a man came to our door and said he wanted to talk to my boys. I don't know his name but I know he works for the mine operator. He told my sons if they wanted to save their father's job they were to burn down your clinic. Everyone around here knew about the letter that lawyer down your way sent to the mine people. Also, there was that article in your paper about inadequate procedures concerning mine operations which they have seen."

"Wow. I did not know we would cause all this trouble trying to help someone. Where are your sons now?"

"They were sent away. The mine people got them jobs, I heard somewhere around Chicago. In case of a lawsuit they didn't want any witnesses available. I worry if the law ever brought them back to testify that would never be allowed."

"I am sorry for your troubles Mrs. Platt and I appreciate you telling me all this. We have repaired the damage to the clinic, and we are not planning any legal action. It would be too expensive and hard to prove who started the fire anyway. We hold no malice toward your sons especially now that I know the circumstances."

Thanking Mrs. Platt again they left and went to his car to leave. Only to find both tires on the driver's side flat with ripped sidewalls.

"Doctor, I fear I have invited you to more troubles coming here, but no one will harm you while I am with you" Anthony said.

"I will call a friend of mine who has a garage to come and haul us to his place of business." Anthony went back to the Platt house and made the call.

While the new tires were being installed Harrell called Lisa Ann to tell her of his day and what he had learned.

"Harrell get in your car and come home. You are a doctor not a detective or a lawyer."

Harrell drove Anthony home and was met as he got out of the car by Mrs. Mauro with a large wax paper package of blackberry cobbler to take home.

"I must call you sometime to get the recipe for your cobbler that Anthony tells me is world class."

"I have no recipe I just throw things together like my mother did. It was never written down." She smiled.

Harrell drove home with an eye on the rear-view mirror to see if he was being followed. He felt better when he crossed over into Tennessee.

In time things settled down and the clinic was rebuilt. Over the months and years as their medical practice grew they were required to hire another doctor and a nurse. Margaret had retired but not before she trained another lady on details of insurance processing and other duties. When Hazel was 5 she had a baby sister Peggy Ann. Again, Lisa Ann stayed with the baby for a few months before returning to work. Life had hit that normal middle-aged period where things seemed to stabilize into a routine. Lisa and Harrell even found time to jog around the high school track as release from the day. Sometimes Hazel Marie went with them, and they would pretend to race with her.

Sometimes as they were jogging Harrell would reiterate for Lisa Ann the days when he and Billy Craft used to race and about how they enjoyed the competition and friendship. He laughed telling her how both were sure they would race in the Olympics.

"We would discuss life, religion, the Olympics, whatever. Two uninformed young philosophers solving the world's problems." Harrell laughed remembering.

"We used to argue over religion and fate and were at two different ends of the spectrum regarding life's journey."

"What was your view on fate?" Lisa asked.

"We were at opposite ends regarding fate. Billy believed that fate predetermined our journey. I said God gave us free will and we determined our journey, not fate."

"Do you suppose there is something in our body makeup that guides us to some predetermined end?" Lisa wondered elongating the discussion.

"You should have married Billy, not me." Harrell laughed.

"Harrell, fate determined we should marry." Now she had him going.

"How could one of our little chromosomes guide us through all our twists and turns and position us to meet at a predetermined point?" Harrell responded.

"Well, what about salmon fry that migrate from their little stream out into the ocean, spend years swimming in all directions, and then return to the very stream where they were born? Isn't that their fate? Was that based on fate or free will?" Lisa continued.

"An interesting point but I think I have read that it has something to do with magnetic waves or magnetic rivers that guide them there."

"Maybe fate will guide you and Billy to meet one day."

"I would like that. He would say it was fate that brought us together. I will say free will brought us there. Enough on this subject."

He had developed many friends over the years, but Billy had been different, somehow, they just meshed.

"Harrell, I have been thinking about the future specifically for the girls. The clinic is doing well financially and there is still some funds from your inheritance. We should do some investing for the future." Lisa Ann said one evening.

"Yes, I agree. Being doctors does not qualify us as savvy investors. We need to study up some in that area, get some help."

"I bet Dan Howard knows a financial planner, or we could attend those clinics where they pitch various financial options. We should call Dan."

"Yes, we need to get serious about our family's future."

Chapter Fifteen

Bill and Mariel had settled into their life in the state university town. Mariel had finished her medical studies and was now working as a medical technician at the university hospital and Bill (no longer Billy) had completed his degree in finance and had begun working for a company building creative iron work, special fences, customized large and decorative gates, etc. for local companies and private property owners. The financial department consisted of three individuals, Bill and two others, Phil Simpson and Harmon Davis. Phil was the youngest of the three, unmarried and nervously excited in his first job. Harmon had been there the longest, and like Bill married. He survived on sarcasm about his job and the company.

The owner of the company was a man named Walters. He was a no-nonsense boss with little in the way of friendly conversations. He seemed to think morning hellos were a waste of everyone's time. He expected his balance sheet to be current and paid close attention to the details therein. Periodically he would hand Bill a handwritten invoice and tell Bill to enter it as paid.

"I need to know the recipient of the payment for the ledger Mr. Walters." Bill once said to him.

"It is a charitable contribution by the company. Just show it as a cash payment." This was said so forcefully that when he received similar items later, he did as told and didn't question the details. As a financial analyst he felt the process strange and wondered if it could withstand an audit.

Bill mentioned it one day to Harmon. "Does this seem strange to you, the way Walters hands us a handwritten invoice and says enter it? How could we or he explain it if questioned by an auditor?"

"If the old man wants to tap dance on a slippery slope, I will just turn my head and laugh when he falls on his ass." Harmon laughed.

"He feels as the boss he is not required to explain his actions to us. I know I questioned him once or twice about irregularities in outgoing payments for raw material or inventories and was given the Walters stare." Phil added.

"Don't bother asking him to go out for a beer." Laughed Harmon. As the senior of the three he had adjusted to the irregularities of old man Walters as they called him; out of his hearing.

"Why do you think he is so secretive about some of his actions? I wonder if we could withstand an audit." Bill went on.

"Not a problem. His bother in law is the auditor. If his sister wants to keep eating regularly the audit will be fine." Harmon added wryly.

Bill continued to think about the way Walters ran the business, but he too needed food for he and Mariel. It was his first job after discharge and he was determined to do a good job and not get involved in company politics.

Donna Atkins the boss's secretary once told Bill about being scolded for picking up an addressed envelope off his desk to mail. Donna, a widow, was known to be inquisitive (Harmon used the term nib shit) about all things, was attuned to all the company gossip. Donna knew who was pregnant and who was the probable father to be, who was stealing office supplies, etc. Not much occurred in the company that escaped Donna's attention.

Donna said Walters grabbed the letter from her and said he would mail it.

"Who was it addressed to?" Bill asked.

"He grabbed it from me so fast I couldn't see." she told Bill.

Bill's curiosity kept him alert for what or to who Walters was sending company money, what charity. He periodically went to Walter's office to discuss a matter and one day saw an addressed envelope on his desk. Being careful not to seem overly curious he looked at the recipient's name as he talked to Walters. It was the Abraham Lincoln School. Well, that answered the question about the charitable organization, though he had never heard of that school. Why then not enter the charity's name in the company ledger?

One day when Walters was away from the plant discussing a large potential order, the office group relaxed for the infrequent coffee and chats. Only when he was away would this little klatch meet for talk and gossip.

"Why is the old man so secretive about many of the financial dealings of the company." Bill asked the assembled group."

"In knowledge and secrets there is power." Harmon suggested. "When he knows something you don't he holds the power. Powerful people have used that weapon for centuries."

"Why doesn't he want it known that the company is donating to charity? That is acceptable in any audit and would be applauded." Bill was still puzzled. "Who in the hell is the Abraham Lincoln School?' Did you all ever hear of it?"

None of the 4 gathered with their coffee had heard of that school.

"I have seen correspondence of some type addressed to the school on his desk from time to time." Harmon added.

"There is some mail he posts himself instead of having me take care of it. I wonder if he has a secret lover." Donna added with a smile.

That brought a roar from Harmon. "Is Gravel Girty still alive? I can see the two of them on a date holding hands, neither one smiling, just looking like world had ended." Harmon continued to laugh.

"I don't think we should criticize Mr. Walter's making a donation to a school." Phil added, just in case Walter's had placed hidden recorders in the office.

Bill decided when home to would look up the Abraham Lincoln School and see where they were and what they taught. After dinner and discussing the Walter's behavior with Mariel he decided to go to the university library to do some research. Combing through a book listing all US colleges and universities he discovered it was characterized as a communist leaning school. Further searching lead him to an article that The House Unamerican Activities Committee described the school as a front for supporting communism. There was no proof offered for this assessment though they said proof existed. Bill had heard some of the Senator McCarthy hearings but hadn't followed all the details. He had been overseas for 2 years and had not paid much attention to politics.

His knowledge of politics was what he heard from his parents as a boy. To them FDR was the savior of the country. He could have carved the holy grail out of granite with a pen knife and they would not be surprised. Face Hyde Park and bow three times. Bill voted for IKE the first time he ran, but he would never tell mom and dad.

If the charges by McCarthy and his followers were true Walters did not want his name subjected to the scrutiny of the McCarthy bunch, hence the contribution from the company not from him. Bill was in a quandary. He was a patriot but believed in free speech and didn't know that much about communism. Should he report Mr. Walter's contribution to the party or forget it? Maybe the donation was legal, if so why hide it? Perhaps he didn't want his employees to know fearing they might publicly release that information?

After discussing his quandary with Mariel, she provided the solution. She had been raised with fear and hatred of the communists. She told him to resign from the company and he did. He told his fellow employees his reason for resigning knowing the reason would eventually reach Walters probably by Donna. He steeled himself expecting a threat of a lawsuit from Walters for defamation, but none came. Thus ended his first working venture into civilian life. Bill was thinking if his fate was waiting for him it was sure taking a few switchbacks.

* * * * *

As promised he had taken Mariel back to her home in Germany for a nice 2-week visit. He also took a bottle of brandy for her father. It was a nice visit for Mariel to reunite with her family and old friends, and they went to the Café several times to eat. Mrs. Vanderhoreven welcomed them and cooked all of Mariel's favorite dishes. Mariel had acclimated to their life in the US, and while enjoying the trip, was anxious to get back to her new home.

Bill and Mr. Vanderhoueven sipped the brandy and talked of politics, religion, and other world changes each evening.

"You only brought one bottle?" He chided smiling.

"Sip slowly sir."

After 2 weeks that Mariel enjoyed immensely, and with tearful goodbyes it was back to the US.

Bill had enjoyed his first job since leaving service but working for Mr. Walters was not always a pleasant experience and when the communist issue arose he had taken Mariel's advice and left. He had enjoyed working with numbers, but he felt like a spigot just spitting out what was asked. He wanted a change.

"What do you want to do, go back to the farm?"

"No, we can't make a living farming now that you are pregnant. We need to have our own business, something with a future."

"I can tell you have been thinking about something. Want to share?"

"I have been thinking of studying to get qualified to be a CFP (certified financial planner). I think it will be more interesting and if someday I opened my own business, it could give us a secure future."

"Well, you have the educational background for that. Can you work on the qualification process while still working? Maybe get a part time job while going go to school."

"Yes, there are CFP evening classes I can take locally. I think I could get work substitute teaching."

Their new future began. It only took Bill a few months to take the series of courses and then study for the CFP exam which he easily passed. With his new CFP in hand, he applied and was accepted by a local agency that provided financial planning for several of the university faculty and to other individuals locally.

Young George Rolf Craft was born, named after his two grandfathers. Now there was an additional reason to plan for the future. Young George's feet hardly touched the ground. Mariel wanted to hold him constantly. She quit her job at the hospital and would stay home with him until he was kindergarten age.

"When George is older, I will buy him a cow and teach him how to milk. Then we will always have free milk." Bill teased.

"Where will you keep it, in the living room?" was Mariel's response.

"Just for a little while until we buy our farm."

"Still thinking about the farm? No, the cow will sleep in the spare bedroom near you."

"Okay, so no cow, maybe a pony."

"Bill change George while I fix dinner."

Finally, after 3 years, Bill became a partner in the agency. There were only two other CFPs in the agency, but others in the company helped with research and planning. To expand their business, they periodically rented a hotel conference room and gave free lectures on financial planning. The intent was to interest attendees in investing and have them come to prepare an investment portfolio. They travelled to other cities made their presentation and handed out brochures and business cards to each conference attendee. Each of the three took turns travelling to nearby towns renting the hotel space and putting out advertising for the free presentation. It was a process that had been successful in expanding their business. Bill thought the next time he had to go on one of these trips he would take Mariel and George now that he was big enough to travel.

When Bill's turn came for a trip he made the arrangements at a hotel including renting a conference room. He also placed an ad in the local papers telling of the free presentation. They would stay 2 nights at the hotel; he made those reservations also. It would be good for Mariel to get away and not have to fix meals. The first full day after arriving Bill would make his presentation hoping to interest some new investors, then they could relax eat dinner and get a good night's sleep before heading home.

The advertising flyers had been previously sent out to the hotel, adds had been placed in the local paper, and posters were put up in the lobby. Bill would begin his presentation at 10 AM. He hoped for one hundred attendees but would be happy to have fifty. As he walked to the lectern and prepared his slides some people were already seated, others standing talking together. It looked to be 35 or 40 attendees.

He began with an opening greeting as 2 or 3 more straggled in. Bill began to talk about the need for a long-term savings and investment plan. He described stocks and bonds and real estate or a combination as ways to diversify a portfolio. He spoke of the diversity offered inherent in mutual funds and exchange traded funds. He described the difference between corporate bonds and municipal bonds. He emphasized the need to determine one's tolerance for risk in deciding on the investment options. He discussed the pros and cons of each type of investment. Finally, after about an hour he closed and opened the floor to questions. A man in the rear raised his hand. He was a tall gentleman starting to grey wearing glasses.

"Yes sir, your question?"

The man stood and said, "How fast can you run the 1600 meters?"

"Wh huh?" Bill took a few steps closer to the questioner.

"I asked how fast can you run the 1600 meters?"

Bill could not believe what he was seeing, a tear started to form as he went quickly forward.

"Two tenths of a second faster than you." He now rushed forward and grabbed Harrell in a bear hug.

Some people stared. A few on their way out stopped and looked. A few clapped for they knew they were witnessing the reunion of two old friends.

"Sit right there. Do not move until I finish here." Bill demanded.

He went back to the lectern to answer additional questions. *Will these questions never end*. An hour later he could not remember the questions or his answers. He sat with Harrell as a million questions formed in his brain.

"Let's go to my room, we have a lot of catching up to do." Bill almost demanded.

"Let us go to my room. I have a suite and my wife and daughters are there." Harrell responded.

"My wife and son are here also. I will get them and we will meet in your suite."

In Harrell's suite the introductions were made with hugs all around. Lisa Ann and Mariel sat together with the three children discussing the children and their lives. Bill and Harrel were asking questions of each other faster than either could answer. They talked about running against each other, the fun they had when together, and their lives over the past years. Bill told them about his mother and father and the farm, and his father's passing, and asked about Harrell's family. Harrell relayed the news about his father's passing and that his mother lived with his sister Amy on the farm.

"Well, my friend should we attribute this reunion to fate or to chance?" Reviving a long-ago discussion, Bill asked smiling.

"I am here of my own free will." Harrell responded smiling.

"Ah yes, now I remember you, often in error never in doubt." Bill responded

"Fate or free will, perhaps a little of each?"

"I find that suggestion acceptable." Harrell laughed as they talked on.

"Age does not seem to have taught you wisdom as is commonly believed. Your wisdom has lain dormant these many years unenlightened by time." Harrell added.

"My dear friend wisdom is acquired not with age but when one closes his mouth and opens his ears and eyes."

Both continued their verbal battles developed long ago and still fresh in both minds. Old remembrances were relived, and they did not want to stop. They also tried to fill in the gaps since last they met cramming their lives into a few sentences.

"Oh, oh "Lisa Ann suddenly remarked to Mariel. "You must go hear this." She had just heard the magic word "liar".

"When I asked about Amy you said her husband was a liar." Bill asked puzzled.

"Biggest liar in the state. He has a certificate to prove it," was Harrell's response.

"Doesn't sound like you think much of Amy's husband."

"Nothing could be further from your assumption; John is the best."

"Do you want to explain?"

"Okay Harrell quit teasing, tell them the story. I know you are dying to." Lisa prodded.

"Well, some background first." Harrell began.

"Amy worked as one of the mangers in a pharmaceutical company and the big boss invited them all to attend a retreat together for a week. It was one of those places where you do tug of war, three legged races, sing-alongs, you know, for team building. One night at a campfire John (who was a stranger to all) was invited to come and tell how he had won the contest for the biggest liar in the state."

"I will now tell the story in first person, as well as I can remember it." Harrell said and began.

"I was born and lived on Lake Oswego down state. All of us boys fished in that lake almost every day. There was a continuing argument over who had caught the biggest fish or who had caught the most fish, always arguing about who was the best angler. After weeks of this it was decided to have a tournament to see who was the best fisherman. All of us put money in a pool and when we counted it we decided that the winner would get $200 and a 6-horsepower outboard motor.

Well, when the day of the tournament arrived, I had a little secret. The day before I had caught a big old snapping turtle in one of my traps. I told the turtle that I would set him free if he would help me catch fish in the tournament, he agreed. It didn't occur to me that once I let him out of the trap he was free to just leave, but he was an honorable turtle and agreed to help me. We began the tournament and the turtle would locate a school of fish and grab the biggest one and bring it to the boat where I would put it in the live well. Occasionally the fish was too small I would make him return it, which did not always please the turtle. But we fished on through the day, and my friends that turtle kept supplying me with large fish.

Finally, the horn blew signaling the end of the tournament, so I started to crank up the outboard to head back to the dock. The motor would not start no matter how often I tried. It was about a mile and a half back to the dock and I told the turtle he would have to tow the boat. The turtle grabbed the tow rope in his mouth and started to pull but we were not making any headway, so I told the turtle to roll over on his back and use the back stroke to pull us in. Well, the turtle began that back stroke, kicking those short little legs, and with me giving encouragement we inched our way back to the dock arriving just at nightfall. When all the fish were weighed and measured, I was declared the winner. As agreed I took the $200 and gave the 6-horsepower outboard to the turtle."

Bill laughed, Mariel laughed, Lisa Ann laughed, and Harrell laughed louder than all.

Then Harrell regaled Mariel and Lisa Ann with Bill's ineptitude on the golf course that day. Bill retaliated with Harrell' pathetic attempt at milking old Bessie. Everyone had a good laugh.

"Bill it's hard to believe this all began with us running in circles around a track." Harrell was remembering.

"Not a circle my friend, an ellipse." Bill corrected

"What's the difference?"

"Well as a demented mathematician once said: "A circle has no corners and an ellipse has no corners too but not nearly so many no corners as a circle."

"Whew."

* * * * *

After a day and a half of a blessed of reunion they all agreed to meet at Amy's farm to visit her and John. She had horses they could ride, and she had a pony that the three children could ride with help for the two smallest. They chose a date a month hence to meet there. Bill was beside himself waiting for the date.

Amy greeted them all with a big hug and introduced her husband John to Bill and Mariel. Bill was a happy to see Mrs. Forsythe after so many years. She was as gracious as ever and commented on Mariel's great beauty and little George's handsome face. A normal fussing over the three children followed with the enthusiasm that children must reluctantly endure.

"Come on folks let us go to the barn. The children are anxious to ride the pony. Hazel Marie has asked Lisa Ann about it every day since she knew we were coming." Harrell interrupted the conversation. They all adjourned to the barn.

Each child took a ride with John walking beside the pony holding on to the bridle and steadying the rider as needed. Then they took more rides and did not want to quit.

"Come on old hayseed let's saddle up the horses and ride off into the sunset." Harrell suggested to Bill.

"No, not me I am too old and would probably fall off and break my leg." Bill answered.

"No problem, I am a doctor. I can fix that."

"You would probably twist my leg backwards and I would walk in circles for the rest of my life."

"Circles or ellipses?"

"This time it is circles. Try to keep up Harrell."

"Don't they ever stop?" Mariel laughed

"Not since they reunited." Lisa Ann offered

"Two middle aged men should never have that much fun together." Mariel added.

www.ingramcontent.com/pod-product-compliance
Lightning Source LLC
Chambersburg PA
CBHW070837160726
48004CB00001B/414
9798891275393